DECK THE HALLS WITH LOVE

Also by Lorraine Heath

Fiction
Lord of Temptation
She Tempts the Duke
Waking up With the Duke
Pleasures of a Notorious Gentleman
Passions of a Wicked Earl
Midnight Pleasures With a Scoundrel
Surrender to the Devil
Between the Devil and Desire
In Bed With the Devil
Just Wicked Enough
A Duke of Her Own
Promise Me Forever
A Matter of Temptation
As an Earl Desires
An Invitation to Seduction
Love With a Scandalous Lord
To Marry an Heiress
The Outlaw and the Lady
Never Marry a Cowboy
Never Love a Cowboy
A Rogue in Texas

DECK THE HALLS WITH LOVE

A Lost Lords of Pembrook Novella

LORRAINE HEATH

AVON IMPULSE
An Imprint of HarperCollins Publishers

Excerpt from *Lord of Wicked Intentions* copyright © 2013 by Jan Nowasky.

Excerpt from *Nights of Steel* copyright © 2012 by Nico Rosso.

Excerpt from *Alice's Wonderland* copyright © 2012 by Allison Dobell.

Excerpt from *One Fine Fireman* copyright © 2012 by Jennifer Bernard.

Excerpt from *There's Something About Lady Mary* copyright © 2012 by Sophie Barnes.

Excerpt from *The Secret Life of Lady Lucinda* copyright © 2012 by Sophie Barnes.

EPub Edition DECEMBER 2012 ISBN: 9780062219336

Print Edition ISBN: 9780062219343

10 9 8 7 6 5

CHAPTER ONE

Pembrook Manor
Yorkshire
December 1858

Standing alone beside a window a short distance away from the midst of the gaiety, Alistair Wakefield, the Marquess of Chetwyn, slowly sipped the Scotch that he had pilfered from his host's library on his way to the grand salon. He'd known that attending this holiday gathering at the Duke and Duchess of Keswick's new country manor would be unpleasant, but then he was not in the habit of shying away from the distasteful. It was the reason that on the morning he was to be married, he had encouraged his bride to seek out her heart's desire. He'd known his being abandoned at the altar would be cause for gossip, that he would be considered weak and inadequate, but he didn't much give a damn. He believed in love, and he'd recognized that Lady Anne Hayworth had given her affections to Lord Tristan Easton. So he'd willingly granted her the freedom to go, and then with as much dignity as possible he'd set about bearing the brunt of what many considered a humiliating affair.

From his shadowed corner, he now watched Lady Meredith Hargreaves dance with *her* betrothed, Lord Litton. Based on her smile and the way her gaze never strayed from his, she appeared to be joyous and very much in love with the fellow. Although perhaps she was simply imbued with the spirit of the season. He could always hope.

He knew he should look about for another dance partner. The problem was that she was the only one with whom he wished to waltz. Hers were the only eyes into which he longed to gaze, hers the only fragrance he yearned to inhale, hers the only voice he wanted whispering near his ear as passion smoldered.

It had been that way for some time now, but he had fought back his burgeoning desire for her out of a sense of obligation and duty, out of a misguided attempt to make amends regarding his younger brother, Walter, who had sacrificed his life in the Crimea. Chetwyn was destined to pay a heavy price for trying to assuage his conscience, unless he took immediate steps to rectify the situation. Lady Meredith was scheduled to marry a few days after Christmas. The decorated tree in the parlor, the sprigs of holly scattered about, and the red bows on the portraits that had greeted him upon his arrival had served as an unwarranted reminder that the auspicious morning was quickly approaching, and then she would be lost to him forever.

But if she loved Litton, could he deny her what he had granted Anne: a life with the man she loved?

It was a quandary with which he struggled, because he wished only happiness for Lady Meredith, but he was arrogant enough to believe that he could bring her joy as no one else could. No other gentleman would hold her in such high esteem. No other man would adore her as he did. Convincing her that she belonged with him was going to be quite the trick, as he suspected she'd rather see him rotting in hell than standing beside her at the altar.

Despite the fact that she was engaged to marry, he kept hoping that she would glance over, would give him a smile, would offer any sort of encouragement at all. Instead she waltzed on, as though for her he no longer existed.

Lady Meredith Hargreaves, the Earl of Whitscomb's daughter, absolutely loved to waltz. Quite honestly, she enjoyed any sort of physical activity. She had loved running, jumping, skipping, and climbing trees until her father had sent her to a ladies' finishing school, where they had taught her that if she did not stifle her enthusiasm for the outdoors, she would never marry. So stifle she did with a great deal of effort and the occasional slap of the rod against her palm.

But dancing was acceptable, and because she was known for being charming—which was no accident—she never lacked for dance partners. She didn't care if they were married, old, young, bent. She didn't care if their eyes were too small, their noses too large, and they stammered. She didn't care if their clothes were not the latest fashion, their skills at interesting conversation nonexistent. When they swept her over the dance floor, she adored every single one of them. And well they knew it.

It showed in her eyes, her smile, and the way she beamed at them. She made them feel as though they mattered, and for those few moments they mattered a great deal because of the pleasure they brought her. But dancing with a lady did not mean that a gentleman wished to marry her. Because she was also known for being quite stubborn, strong-willed, and prone to arguing a point when most ladies would simply smile and pretend that they hadn't the good sense to know their own minds.

She did know hers, and therefore she knew without question that Lord Litton was the man for her. He often praised her strong points. He sent her flowers. He wrote her poetry. He danced with her, a daring four times the night they met. Four, when only two times was acceptable. He had told her that he simply couldn't deny himself the pleasure of her presence.

His inability to resist her was what had led to them being caught the night of Greystone's ball in the garden in a very compromising situation that had resulted in a rather hasty betrothal. Her father had managed to limit the damage done by ensuring that no one other than he and her brothers knew of the discovery. Litton had been quick to propose on the spot, but then her father could be quite intimidating. As they were discovered before they had moved beyond a kiss, the wedding was not being rushed. Meredith knew Litton was an honorable man. He could have run off, but he didn't. He stood by her and offered to marry her. She didn't like the little niggle of doubt that surfaced from time to time and made her wonder if he arranged to be caught. If he did, was it because he so desperately wanted *her* or her dowry?

As he smiled down on her now, she sent the irritating doubts to perdition and accepted that he was madly in love with her. They would be wondrously happy together. If only her heart would cooperate.

She did wish she hadn't noticed when Lord Chetwyn had strolled laconically into the room before the strains of the first dance had started. Based upon what had happened in the church earlier in the year, she hadn't expected him to make an appearance where he would be forced to encounter his former fiancée and her husband. Lord Tristan was, after all, the Duke of Keswick's twin brother, so Chetwyn had to know that he couldn't avoid them. But he had cut such a fine figure in his black tailcoat as he had greeted his host and hostess. His fair complexion stood out next to the duke's black hair and bronzed skin. His blond hair was perfectly styled, but even from a distance Meredith had seen the ends curling. She suspected by midnight the strands would be rebelling riotously, and he would no doubt be searching for some lady to run her fingers through them in order to tame them. She had once considered performing the service herself when they had taken a turn about a park. Thank goodness, she'd not been that foolish. It would have hurt all the more when he began to give his attentions to Lady Anne.

He was now standing in a corner, coming into view from time to time as though she were riding on a carousel, rather than swirling over a dance floor in Litton's arms. Even when she couldn't see him, she could sense Chetwyn's gaze lighting upon her as gently as a lover's caress. She had once thought that he might ask for her hand. But he had moved on, and so had she.

Litton was as fair, but his hair would not be misbehaving by the end of the evening. She rather wished it would. She longed for an excuse to run her fingers through it, although she suspected he might be rather appalled to know the direction of her thoughts. He did not have as easy a grin as Chetwyn, but his seriousness was endearing. She only wished he would reclaim the passion that had resulted in a near scandal.

"You've drifted away again," Litton said quietly.

"I'm sorry. I was just noticing how the snow is growing thicker beyond the windows." A small lie, but she rather doubted that he would welcome knowing that Chetwyn was occupying her thoughts.

"Yes, we're in for quite a storm tonight, I think. I hope we shall all be able to travel home when the time comes."

"I'm sure we will."

"You're such an optimist. It's one of the things I love about you."

Touched by his comment, she squeezed his shoulder. "We shall be happy together, won't we?"

"Immeasurably."

The music drifted into silence. He lifted her gloved hand to his lips. "As your card is filled and you're gracing other lords with your presence for a while, I'm going to the gaming room for a bit. Just remember the last dance is mine."

"I would never give it to anyone else."

Watching him walk away, she could not help but think that she was a most fortunate lady indeed. Then she looked over and saw her next dance partner approaching.

Lord Wexford smiled. He was a handsome enough fellow, recently returned from a trip to Africa. Bowing slightly, he took her hand. "My dance, I believe."

"Quite. I've been looking forward to it."

"Not as much as I have. The last lady with whom I danced is not yet spoken for, and she was quite adept at listing her wifely qualities as though she were delivering a shopping list."

Meredith was familiar enough with Lady Beatrix's habits to know that Wexford was speaking of her. Bless Lady Beatrix, but she seemed to think that if she didn't point out her good qualities, no gentleman would discover them. She had such little faith in the observational powers of the males of the species.

"Did you know that she is so talented with her sewing that she can weave twenty stitches into an inch of cloth?" Lord Wexford asked. "I am sure it is quite an impressive feat, but as I've never taken the time to measure and count stitches—"

"My lord?"

Wexford spun around. Lord Chetwyn stood there, extending a small slip of paper toward him, and Meredith's heart beat out an unsteady tattoo. She had vainly hoped with so many guests in attendance that she might avoid encountering him entirely. It wasn't that she was cowardly, but she reacted in the strangest fashion when he was near—as though she were on the cusp of swooning.

He smelled of bergamot, a scent she could no longer inhale without thinking of him. Thank goodness Litton smelled of cloves. Harsh, not particularly appealing, but it didn't matter. Nothing about him reminded her of Chetwyn, which made him perfect in every way.

"I'm sorry to interrupt you," Chetwyn murmured as music once again began to fill the ballroom, "but a lady asked me to deliver this to you as discreetly as possible. She said it was quite urgent."

Meredith couldn't help but think that Chetwyn didn't comprehend the term "discreet." He should have secreted Wexford away or waited until the dance was over. She would have preferred the latter.

Wexford furrowed his brow. "Which lady?"

"She asked me not to say. I think she desired to remain a bit mysterious, but I was given reason to believe you were . . . well acquainted."

Wexford opened the note, then smiled slowly. "Yes, I see." He turned to Meredith. "I fear I must attend to this matter."

"Of course. I hope all is well."

"Couldn't be better."

And with that he was gone. Staring after him, she was certain he would be rendezvousing with the woman, whoever she was.

"I would be honored to stand in his stead," Lord Chetwyn said. Then, as though she had acquiesced, he was leading her onto the dance floor.

"I fear I'm no longer of a mind to dance. I thought to get some refreshment. Alone."

"Surely, you would not pass up your favorite tune."

"Greensleeves." He remembered. The first dance they'd ever shared was to this song. She had gazed up at his sharp, precise, patrician features and decided that he would age well, for there was nothing about him that would sag with time. He was one of those fortunate gentlemen upon whom the gods of heredity smiled kindly. She had been smiling upon him as well, giddy at his nearness, excited by his attentions. She thought she might have fallen a little bit in love with him during that first encounter. "Chetwyn—"

"One dance, Merry."

"Please don't call me that. It's far too personal, too informal." But she didn't object when he took her into his arms and glided her over the floor. She hated that he was such a marvelous dancer, that he exuded confidence, and that he made her feel as though only the two of them were moving about the room. Everyone else receded into the woodwork. Everyone else ceased to matter.

Giving herself a mental shake, she refused to succumb to his charms once again. She could be distant, pretend indifference, give the impression that he had never been more than a dance partner.

"Rather fortunate timing that Wexford received a note before this particular song started," she said pointedly. Did his eyes have to hold hers as though they were examining a precious gift?

"Not really. The note was from me, you see. Although he doesn't know that, as it was unsigned."

She didn't know whether to be angry or flattered. "You took a chance with that ploy. How did you know he would not question an unsigned note from a lady?"

"All gentlemen welcome notes from mysterious ladies suggesting a tryst in the garden."

Her eyes widened. "But it's storming out there."

"As I'm well aware, but I'm not familiar enough with the residence to know where else to send him."

"What if he freezes to death?"

"I don't think that's likely to happen. He strikes me as being fairly intelligent. I'm sure he'll head back in once he gets too cold and the lady doesn't show."

She studied him for half a moment before it dawned on her. "You purposely stole his dance."

"I did. I saw all the gentlemen circling you earlier, so I knew your dance card was filled. And if it wasn't filled, I rather doubted that you would take pleasure in scribbling my name—"

"I do not scribble."

He grinned. Why did he have to have such an infectious smile that begged her to join him?

"I'm sure you don't. Forgive me, Meredith, but I wanted a moment with you, and I didn't think you would be likely to meet me in a garden. Not after our last meeting among the roses."

Inwardly she cringed at the reminder of when he had informed her that he would be asking Lady Anne to marry him. "I thought you should know," he'd said quietly, as though Meredith cared, as though he knew she'd pinned her hopes on him. When those hopes had come unpinned among the roses, her heart had very nearly shattered. Thank goodness she was made of stern stuff. She'd taken a good deal of satisfaction in the fact that her voice had not trembled when she'd replied, "I wish you the very best." Then she had strolled away with such aplomb that she had considered going onto the stage. What a scandal becoming an actress would cause, and the one thing her father could not abide was scandal.

Yet Chetwyn had found himself in the midst of one that still had the ladies wagging their tongues. Lord Tristan was seen as a heroic romantic for claiming his love on the day she was to marry another, and Chetwyn was viewed as that unfortunate Lord Chetwyn. She decided she could be gracious.

"I'm sorry that things did not go as you'd planned for yourself and Lady Anne."

"I'm not sorry at all. I'm happy for her. Do you love him?" he asked, taking her aback with his abrupt question. They were supposed to be talking about him, not her. If he wasn't holding her so firmly, she thought she might have flown out of his arms.

"You say that, my lord, as though there is but one *him* in my life when there are several. My father, my brothers—there are five of them, you know—my uncles, cousins—"

"Litton," he cut in, obviously not at all enchanted by her little game.

"It seems a rather pointless question. I favor Viscount Litton immensely. I'd not be marrying him otherwise."

She could not mistake the look of satisfaction that settled into his deep brown eyes, as though she'd revealed something extraordinary. "Favoring is not love."

"I'll not discuss my heart with you." *Not when you'd once come so close to holding it, and then set it aside with so little care.*

"I don't know that you'll be happy with him."

She straightened her shoulders, angled her chin. "You're being quite presumptuous."

"You require a man of passion, one who can set your heart to hammering. Is he capable of either of those things?" His eyes darkened, simmered, captured hers with an intensity that made it impossible to look away. Her mouth went dry.

Ignoring his question, she released an awkward-sounding laugh. "You think *you* are?"

"I know I am. Within your gloves, your palms are growing damp."

Blast it! That was where all the moisture in her mouth had gone. How did he know?

"Your breaths are becoming shorter. Your cheeks are flushed." He lowered his gaze, her nipples tautened. Whatever was the matter with her? Then he lifted his eyes back to hers. "Correction. All your skin is flushed."

"Because I'm dancing. It's warm in here."

"It's the dead of winter. Most women are wearing shawls."

"Only the wallflowers."

"You would never be a wallflower. You are the most exciting woman here. Meet me later. Somewhere private so that we may talk."

"What do you call this current movement of the tongue? Singing?"

"It's too public. We need something more intimate."

An image flashed of him kissing her. She had often wondered at his flavor, but she would not fall for him again, she would not. "For God's sake, I am betrothed."

"As I'm well aware." She saw a flicker of sadness and regret cross his features. "You should know, Merry, that I am here only because of you."

"Your flirtation is no longer welcome, Chetwyn. I shall be no man's second choice."

"You were always my first." His eyes held sincerity and something else that fairly took her breath: an intense longing. Dear God, even Litton didn't look at her like that. Chetwyn's revelation delighted, angered, and hurt at the same time.

She released a bitter laugh. "Well, you had a frightfully funny way of showing it, didn't you?" She stepped away. "If you'll excuse me, I've become quite parched."

Before he could offer to fetch her a flute of champagne, she was walking away. His words were designed to soften her, but she wouldn't allow them to breach the wall she'd erected against him. She was betrothed now. Nothing he said would change that.

For Chetwyn, it was too late. Her course was set. She wished that thought didn't fill her with sorrow.

Chapter Two

Chetwyn discovered that being left at the altar wasn't nearly as humiliating or as infuriating as being abandoned on the dance floor. Or perhaps it simply seemed so because he cared a good deal more about Merry traipsing off without him than he did about Anne.

As people swirled around him, they gave him a questioning glance, an arched eyebrow, pursed lips. Then the whispers began, and he had a strong urge to tell them all to go to the devil.

Wending his way past ballooning hems and dancing slippers, he fought to keep his face in a stoic mask that revealed none of his inner thoughts. He suspected a good many of the women would swoon if they knew that he wanted to rush after Merry, usher her into a distant corner, and kiss her until the words coming from her mouth were sweet instead of bitter. It didn't lessen his anger that she had every right to be upset with him. But then the fury was directed at himself, not her. He'd handled things poorly. He needed to be alone with her to adequately explain, and furthermore to sway her away from Litton. But he could see now that he had misjudged her loyalty to Litton and her dislike of himself.

"Chetwyn?"

Turning, he smiled at the gossamer-haired beauty standing before him. "Anne."

"Is everything all right?"

"Yes, of course." Even as he spoke the words, he realized that had they married, he'd have spent a good deal of his time being untruthful with her, as he was now. He liked her, adored her, in fact, but he didn't love her. He doubted he ever would have fallen for her as Walter had before he left for the Crimea. And certainly not as Lord Tristan had.

"I'm so very glad you came," she said.

"Yes, well, I must thank you for sending me the list of guests who had accepted the invitation."

"I daresay that I needed to send only one name: Lady Meredith."

To imply he was taken aback by the accuracy of her words was an understatement. He thought he was so skilled at hiding his emotions. "How did you know?"

Taking his arm, she guided him over to an assortment of fronds that provided some protection from prying eyes. "While you were courting me, I noticed the way you looked at her with longing on a few occasions when our paths crossed with hers. I thought perhaps she had rebuffed you, which I certainly didn't understand, but after observing the drama on the dance floor, I don't think the rebuffing happened until tonight."

The *drama* that everyone had observed. He thought in public he'd be spared her wrath. Where Merry was concerned, he seemed destined to constantly misjudge. "I'm not quite certain *rebuffed* is the proper word. She is betrothed, after all. What sort of gentleman would I be to try to steal her away from Litton?"

Anne smiled. "A very determined one, I should think, and I would wager on your success." She glanced around as though fearing that she might be overheard. "As you know, my brothers are the worst gossips in all of England. Jameson tells me that Litton is up to his eyebrows in debt to Rafe. While I don't know my brother by marriage very well, Tristan has assured me that Rafe is someone to whom I'd never wish to owe anything."

Chetwyn was of the same mind. Lord Rafe Easton owned a gambling establishment, and while it had a solid reputation, Chetwyn preferred one with a bit more class, better clientele, and no rumors of thuggery surrounding it. "You think Litton is marrying Meredith only for her dowry?"

"I've heard it's substantial. I wish Society would do away with the entire dowry business. It always leaves a lady wondering at a man's true motivations."

"Surely you have no doubt where Lord Tristan is concerned."

She laughed. "Oh, absolutely not. No, my concern is with Lady Meredith. One of my other brothers, and I can't remember which one now, hinted that this betrothal came about under unfortunate circumstances."

Chetwyn felt as though he'd taken a punch to the gut. "You think he compromised her?"

"I don't know. It was something about a garden and witnesses—" She held up her hands. "Dear God, I'm as bad as they are. Forgive me. I know not of what I speak, and so I should not be speaking. I just dislike seeing her with Litton—whom I don't much care for—when she could be with you, whom I favor a great deal."

Reaching out, Chetwyn squeezed her hand. "What matters, Anne, is that she is happy."

"Of course, you're right. It's just that she didn't look as happy with him as she did with you."

He chuckled. "Now I know you're biased. She was quite put out with me the entire time we were dancing."

"I was put out with Tristan a good bit of the time after I met him, but it didn't stop me from falling in love with him." Rising up on her toes, she bussed a quick kiss over his cheek. "I wish you luck with your endeavors here."

As she wandered away, Chetwyn decided that his best course for the moment was to enjoy another glass of Scotch. He was heading toward the doorway when Wexford stepped into his path, his nose red, his cheeks flushed, his eyes radiating panic.

"Who the devil was she?" he asked. "I never saw anyone. She's no doubt wandered off and is in danger of freezing to death by now. We must cease the music, form search parties, call out the hounds."

"Steady, old chap," Chetwyn commanded, placing his hands on Wexford's shoulders, attempting to calm him before damage was done. "There was no woman."

Wexford blinked and stared at him as though he'd spoken in Mandarin. "Whatever do you mean?"

Obviously the man's ability to reason had frozen while he was outside. "I wrote the note. The entire thing was a ruse as I wished to dance that particular dance with Lady Meredith."

"You sent me out in the cold? For a dance? Why didn't you just ask, man?"

"Would you have stepped aside?"

"That is beside the point." Wexford held up a finger. "I shan't soon forget this, Chetwyn." With that ominous warning, he stormed off.

Considering Wexford had once shot a rhinoceros, Chetwyn considered himself fortunate that the veiled threat was quite mild. Then he saw a young lady grinning in the doorway. "I don't suppose it would be my good fortune to discover you're deaf."

With a giggle, she shook her head and disappeared into the hallway. Lovely. More fodder for the gossip mill.

"He sent Lord Wexford out into the storm so he could dance with you," Lady Sophia said.

Meredith had come to the retiring room to regain her calm because it was too early to retire to her chambers. She found herself surrounded by Ladies Sophia, Beatrix, and Violet.

"Terribly romantic," Lady Violet said.

"Terribly selfish," Lady Beatrix insisted. "Wexford could have died."

Meredith wondered if she was hoping for more than a dance from the fellow. She wondered if she should tell Lady Beatrix that she shouldn't strive so hard to impress men with her litany of accomplishments, then wondered if things might have been different if she, herself, had tried harder with Chetwyn—if she had thrown a fit in the garden instead of giving the impression that she could hardly be bothered by his change of heart. Was she as much to blame for their diverging paths as he?

"Perhaps we shall have a duel at dawn," Lady Sophia said, her voice rife with excitement.

"Between Chetwyn and Wexford?" Meredith asked.

"I was thinking more along the lines of Chetwyn and Litton. I daresay it is one thing to dance with a lady, an entirely different matter to go to such great lengths to do so."

"My dance card was filled. He wanted a dance. Make no more of it than that." Even now she should be in the ballroom fulfilling her obligations. Perhaps she would claim a headache.

"It's no secret his family coffers suffer for want of coin. His father made some ghastly investments, from what I hear. He needs an heiress with a substantial dowry. He lost Lady Anne—"

"You say that as though he misplaced her," Meredith interrupted, impatient with the conversation. Standing quickly, she shook out her skirts. She wanted to be more than her dowry to some man. Was she to Litton? She was no longer as sure. "I'm returning to the ballroom."

It was nearing midnight, the last dance would be soon, and she was anxious to see Litton, to have him wash away any lingering evidence that Chetwyn had danced with her. But she waited for him in vain, stood among the older matrons whose hips no longer allowed them the luxury of dance. Her only consolation was that Chetwyn wasn't about to witness her disappointment. She wondered if he'd taken his leave. She could only hope.

CHAPTER THREE

The residence had grown quiet, the only sound the wind howling beyond the windows. Sitting alone in a chair by the fire in the billiards room, Chetwyn savored his Scotch and reminisced about the first time that he'd set eyes on Merry.

For more than a year he'd been in seclusion, grieving the loss of his brother. Finally, the Season before last, Chetwyn had taken the first step out of mourning by attending a ball. He had felt as though he were a stranger in a strange land. All the finery, the food, the laughter, the gaiety—did any of them deserve any of it when so many had died?

Suffocating in that overly flowered ballroom, attempting to talk about weather and theater and books, had made him feel as though his clothing were strangling him. He was merely going through the motions of being present, wishing he'd not been so quick to return to Society.

And then his gaze had landed on Lady Meredith. He was struck with the romantic notion that she was the sort over whom men fought wars. He'd desperately wanted to release her raven hair from its pins. The pink roses that adorned it matched the ones embroidered in her pale pink gown. It had draped off her alabaster shoulders, enticing a man to touch them. She was talking with three other ladies, and then she tilted back her head slightly and laughed. The glorious tinkling had wafted over to him, and for the first time in a good long while he didn't feel dead, didn't feel as though he had been buried alongside Walter. He was ever so glad that he was alive to hear such sweet music.

As though noticing his regard, she looked at him with eyes of clover green, and he had to take a step back to maintain his balance. The force of her was like nothing he'd ever experienced. Initially, he attributed it to being out of the ballrooms for so long, but he slowly came to realize that it was simply the power of her.

Throughout the Season, he danced with her at every opportunity, strolled with her through gardens and parks, sent her flowers and sweets. She returned to her father's estate for the winter. Chetwyn returned to his, but he'd been unable to forget her. She was more than a passing fancy.

Then in early spring a soldier delivered a letter from Walter, long after he was gone. The man hadn't posted it for fear it would become lost on the journey from the Crimea. Walter's words had shaken Chetwyn to the core. As he lay ill, he must have known that the Grim Reaper was hovering nearby, because he asked Chetwyn to promise to ensure that his betrothed was happy. Chetwyn, numbskull that he was, had thought the only way to ensure Lady Anne's well-being was to marry her himself, so he'd held his growing feelings for Lady Meredith in check. When the next Season was upon them, he turned his attentions to securing

Lady Anne's happiness while Lady Meredith slipped beyond reach.

He had no right to ask her for forgiveness, no right to ask for a second chance. She had moved on with her life, she had found another. It was time for him to do the same, to stop living in the past, to stop focusing on what might have been—

If he'd not been so insistent on restoring his estates to their former glory.

If he'd not been hoarding his coins for that purpose rather than giving his brother an allowance so he could live the life of a gentleman.

If he hadn't purchased Walter a commission so he was forced to live the life of a soldier.

If he hadn't read Walter's final letter and allowed it to skew his perspective and overwhelm him with remorse.

It mattered little to him now that Walter had once commented that he enjoyed being in the army, had felt he had gained purpose. He had died as a young man, while Chetwyn would no doubt die as an old one. And without Merry at his side.

He downed the contents of his glass, reached for the bottle he'd set beside the chair, and refilled the tumbler. As the room was beginning to spin and his head was feeling dull, he knew he should be abed, where in sleep he would dream of Merry, of her raven hair and green eyes and the way she had once smiled at him as though he could do no wrong. Yet he had managed to do wrong aplenty.

He barely moved when he heard the door open. Slowly shifting his gaze over, he wondered briefly if he'd already fallen asleep, because there she was in a much simpler dress than she'd been wearing earlier. No petticoats. Possibly no corset. It was designed for comfort, not company. It could also be discarded in a flash if a man were to set his mind to removing it. He had imbibed a bit too much because he was already envisioning the joy he would experience in giving all those buttons their freedom.

Her braided hair fell past her hips, her slippers were plain. Nothing about her was intentionally enticing, and yet he was thoroughly beguiled.

She glanced around warily. He held still, waiting for the moment when she would see him. Only she didn't, and he realized the deep shadows and the angle of the chair hid his presence from her. She swept her gaze around the room once more before returning to the door and closing it with a hushed snick.

He wondered if she was waiting for Litton. Chetwyn thought that if the viscount came through the door, he might very well lose any semblance he had of being a gentleman. He wouldn't stand for it, watching them behave as lovers. It could be the only reason for this late-night tryst, and dammit all to hell, she appeared to be anticipating it. Her eyes took on a glow, her smile was one of someone doing what she ought not to be caught doing. Dear God, help him, but he wanted to kiss those lips, he wanted to be doing things with them that *he* ought not to be doing.

She wandered over to the billiards table and scraped her fingers over the baize top as she slowly walked its length. Against the taut cloth, her nails made a faint raspy sound, and it was all he could do not to groan as he imagined her trailing those fingertips over his chest, circling around his nipples, pinching, leaning in—

She stilled, and his thoughts careened to a stop as though she'd heard them. She glanced over her shoulder, and he feared that he had made a sound. He wasn't quite ready for her to know that he was there. Again, he wondered if she was meeting Litton, if she was going to stretch out on the table for her lover. Would he unravel her hair and spread it across the green? Would he worship her as she deserved to be worshipped?

Chetwyn imagined removing her slippers, kissing her toes, then taking his mouth on a slow, leisurely journey up her calves, over her knees, along her thighs—

Christ! If he carried on with these imaginings, he was going to be unable to stand when Litton showed. If the rumors being bandied about were true, he'd compromised her once in a garden. He wouldn't hesitate to do so here, long after the stroke of midnight, when most were abed and no one was about to interrupt. Chetwyn flexed the fingers not holding the glass. He rather fancied the idea of introducing his fist to Litton's nose.

She fairly skipped over to the rack on the wall and selected a cue stick. Mesmerized, he watched as she tested its weight, twirled it between her fingers, and carried it over to the table. She gathered the balls, racked them; then, cue in hand, she leaned over, presenting him with a rather enticing view of her backside. A tiny voice urged him to stay where he was, to enjoy the unexpected gift of her arrival, but it was such a small voice, easily ignored, and he could enjoy her so much more if no distance separated them.

Unable to hold back his anticipation, he unfolded his body and crept over to where she was carefully positioning her cue.

When he was near enough to smell her rose fragrance, he leaned in and whispered in a low, sensual drawl, "You're doing it all wrong."

With a startled yelp, she flung herself backward, her head smacking soundly into his jaw—

And the world went black.

With her heart pounding, her entire body quaking, Meredith dropped to her knees, more because of their weakened state than the man sprawled on the floor. Had she killed him? Dear God, her father abhorred scandal, and she couldn't think of anything that would set tongues to wagging faster than murder. She could envision herself traipsing toward the gallows with her father berating her the entire way for bringing shame upon the family.

"Chetwyn?" She placed her palm against his cheek, felt the stubble prick her tender flesh, and fought not to compare it to the stiff baize over which she trailed her fingers only moments before. She much preferred the warmth of his skin and the bristles that were thicker than she imagined and a shade darker than his hair. He should have appeared unkempt. Instead he looked very, very dangerous, and something that greatly resembled pleasure settled in the pit of her stomach. Why didn't she ever feel this liquid fire that spread into her limbs when she was in Litton's presence?

She leaned lower and inhaled Chetwyn's bergamot fragrance mingled with Scotch. She considered pressing her lips to his, just for a taste. How often—before he had shifted his attentions to Lady Anne—had she longed for a turn about the garden with him that would have resulted in an illicit kiss? It was her shameful secret, her dark fantasy that in a shadowed part of a garden he would cease to be a gentleman, and she would no longer act as a lady. She had wanted so much with him that she hadn't wanted with other admirers. She wished he hadn't come here, that his presence wasn't reminding her of all her silly imaginings. She wanted to marry Litton, to be his wife, his countess eventually—after his father passed.

Yet, if she were honest with herself, Chetwyn stirred something deep within her that Litton had yet to reach. And that acknowledgment terrified her. Would she make him happy if her thoughts could stray so easily to another?

As he groaned, Chetwyn opened his eyes wide, blinked, and rubbed his jaw. "You've got quite the punch," he muttered.

Now that she saw he was going to be all right, irritation swamped her. "You have a jaw like glass. None of my brothers would have gone down that easily or that hard. It's a wonder you didn't shake the foundation of the residence. What the devil were you doing here, sneaking up on me?"

"It's the gentlemen's room, so the question, sweetheart, is what are you doing here?"

She settled back on her heels, not quite ready to leave until she saw him firmly on his feet, although a small a part of her was wishing she *had* killed him. "Not that it's any of your business, but I was having difficulty falling asleep. I was looking for the library so I might find a book to read."

He had the audacity to give her a wolfish grin that did nothing to settle her riotous thoughts. If anything, it only made her want to kiss him all the more. Whatever was wrong with her?

"But once you realized you weren't in the library, you didn't leave. I think you purposely came here."

"Think what you want." Rising to her feet, she turned to leave.

"Are you meeting someone?" he asked.

She spun back around. "Of course not. I'm a lady. I don't—"

She abruptly cut off her protest. She had been alone with a gentleman, was alone with one now. She knew she should leave, but the truth was that she *had* come here to play billiards. She was quite disappointed that she wouldn't have the opportunity to do so—because of his presence. He did little more than constantly bring disappointment into her life. "I hear that Lord Wexford is quite put out with you."

He shoved himself to his feet. In the shadowed room, he seemed larger, broader, more devastatingly handsome. "Facing his wrath was well worth the dance."

"Who do you think he *thought* he was going to meet?" she asked.

Chetwyn leaned his hip against the table and crossed his arms over his chest. "I haven't a clue. You seem to know more about the gossip than I. Who do you think?"

She shrugged, wondering why she was prolonging her visit. She had always felt most comfortable with him, even when her thoughts had turned down dark corners where they shouldn't. Even now she recalled the feel of him behind her, the warmth of his breath on her neck as he'd whispered in her ear. "I don't know, and I don't suppose it matters. I should go."

"Play billiards with me."

His eyes held a challenge that she knew had little to do with the actual game. He was daring her to stay, to risk being with him. Did he know how much she was drawn to him, how very dangerous he was to her?

"I'll teach you," he said.

She angled her chin haughtily. "I already know how to play. Litton taught me. What do I gain if I win?"

"What would you like?"

"For you to leave immediately."

He furrowed his brow. "The room?"

"The manor, the estate, the shire." She knew the challenge was now in her gaze, and she could see him considering it, perhaps wondering how truly skilled she was.

"And if I win?" he asked, his voice thrumming with an undercurrent that should have frightened her off. "What do I receive?"

"Our last night here there is to be another ball. A dance. Whichever one you want. I shall let you sign my card first."

He picked up her cue stick and studied it as though he were trying to determine how it had been made. "A kiss." He shifted his gaze over to her and captured her as though he'd suddenly wrapped his arms around her. "As soon as I sink my last ball."

"That would be entirely inappropriate."

He gave her a devilish grin. "Which is why I want it."

"You always struck me as quite the gentleman."

A shadow crossed his features. "Not tonight. I've spent too much time contemplating past mistakes. You were one of them, you know. If I had to do it over, I would not have hurt you."

Not exactly what she wanted to hear. If he had it to do over, she wanted him to kiss her madly, passionately in the garden, to court her properly, to perhaps ask for her hand on bended knee. But he had never declared any feelings for her, so she had little right to be hurt. "You overstate your importance to me. A kiss from you will have no effect upon me, so I accept the challenge."

His eyes darkened, and she was left with the impression that she'd made a terrible mistake.

"You may break," he said.

Yes, she thought, she very well might. Her heart, at least. Where he was concerned, it had once been close to shattering. Then she scolded herself. *Silly chit, he was talking about the balls.*

While he went to the wall to examine the selection of cue sticks, she picked up hers, moved to the end of the table, and began to position herself as Litton had taught her.

"Still not quite right," Chetwyn said, his voice coming from near enough that she realized he was no longer at the wall.

She didn't dare give him the satisfaction of glancing over her shoulder to discern exactly where he was, but when she took a deep breath she filled her nostrils with bergamot. Close then, very close indeed. "Oh?"

She was quite pleased that she didn't squeak like a dormouse. Her nerves were suddenly wrung tight, and she couldn't decide if she wanted the satisfaction of besting him or the gaining of the knowledge of what his kiss was like. She didn't know why she was suddenly obsessed with the thought of his mouth on hers. Litton had kissed her, so she knew very well that the pressing of lips left a great deal to be desired. She had always thought there would be heat, but all she'd felt was the cold. Perhaps it was because they had been outside, the evening had been cool, and the arrival of her father and brothers had abruptly ended any stirring of embers.

"Allow me to show you," Chetwyn said.

She was tempted to ignore him and smack the balls, but better to let him believe she knew not what she was doing so her victory would leave him flummoxed and feeling quite the fool. "All right."

She began to straighten.

"No, stay as you are."

She stilled as his arms came around her. Litton certainly hadn't taken this intimate approach to teaching her. He'd not touched her at all. He merely explained the rules in a serious, endearing manner as though he were preparing to submit them to *Hoyle's* to be included in an upcoming edition since the publication had yet to explain how billiards should be played.

As the length of his body nudged against hers, she became acutely aware of the fact that she was wearing little more than her chemise and drawers beneath the dress. After her maid had prepared her for bed and she'd had difficulty finding sleep, she'd wanted to slip into something that she could manage on her own. At home, she would have simply gathered her wrap about her, but one didn't traipse through a guest's home in her nightdress, although now she was questioning the wisdom of doing it with so little to separate her from Chetwyn. His warmth seeped through her clothing to heat her flesh. His large hands closed over hers, and she realized how capable they appeared. He possessed strong, thick fingers with blunt-tipped nails. His roughened jaw teased her neck. His hair tickled her temple. She had been correct with her earlier assessment. It was curling with wild abandon, and she ached to slip her fingers through the feathery strands.

"Relax," he murmured into her ear, and within her slippers her toes curled as though he were giving attention to them.

"I am relaxed." *Liar, liar.*

"You're as stiff as a poker. I'm going to position your hands, your stance."

"I think you're wrong. I think they are exactly as they need to be."

"Not if you wish to beat me."

Turning her head to the side, she met and held his gaze. "Why would you assist me in giving you a sound thrashing and miss out on your kiss? If you truly wanted it—"

"Oh, I truly want it," he said in a silken voice. "And I intend to have it."

Suddenly, one of his hands was cupping her cheek, while his fingers plowed through her hair. He somehow managed to twist and bend her slightly so she was cradled in his other arm. He lowered his head, and his mouth plundered. No soft taking this, but an urgency. He ravished with his tongue as though he would die if he didn't taste her, as though he would cease to exist if he left anything unexplored.

This was exactly what she had imagined kissing him would be like during the months when they had flirted, danced, and strolled about. She had expected heat and passion. She had instinctually known that within him was a smoldering fire that once set ablaze would be difficult to extinguish. Working one hand beneath his waistcoat, she felt the solidness of his muscles beneath the fine linen of his shirt. Wanton that she was, she wanted his coat, waistcoat, and shirt gone. She wanted the feel of his skin against her palms. She wanted to scrape her nails over his bare back.

Guilt slammed into her. She felt none of these things when Litton had kissed her. His had been pleasant, tame, proper. Nothing about Chetwyn was proper at that moment.

His guttural groans reverberated through his chest, vibrated into her. She ran her free hand through his golden locks, felt them wrapping around her fingers as though they intended to hold her captive as easily as his mouth did.

He dragged his lips along her throat, and she found herself arching up toward him, offering him more.

"You haven't won," she said breathlessly. They hadn't even started to play.

Raising his head, he gave her a dark grin. "Oh, but I have."

With as little effort as though she weighed no more than a pillow, he lifted her up and laid her on the billiards table. She was vaguely aware of the balls scattering. Leaning over her, he braced his arms on either side of her head, his gaze intent.

"Don't marry him," he urged, his voice low and sensual until it more closely resembled a caress.

"I have to."

"Because of the kiss in the garden?"

Her heart slammed into her ribs. "What do you know of the garden?"

"Only rumors. The rest of your life shouldn't be determined by a kiss."

Yet here she was thinking that if she weren't betrothed, the kiss he had just delivered would have been the guiding star for the remainder of her life. No one else's would ever measure up.

A broken betrothal ... Litton would sue. Her father wouldn't allow that sort of scandal to happen. "You're being a bit hypocritical. You're asking me to change the direction of my life because you managed to steal a kiss that left me breathless. You had your chance with me, Chetwyn. You chose another. Now so have I."

"I can explain."

"It doesn't matter. You may be in the habit of hurting people, but I'm not." Rolling away from him, she scrambled off the table. "I was handling the cue properly. I would have beaten you, and I think you know it. Please accept that things are over between us."

"Things never really got properly started between us. If we had more time—"

She shook her head, grateful that was all that was required to silence him. So few lamps burned. The fire on the hearth cast dancing shadows around him as he stood tall and straight, but she was left with the impression of someone trapped in hell. "But we don't have the luxury of time, Chetwyn. Christmas is almost here, and then I'll be married shortly after."

Turning on her heel, she marched from the room before he could object. When the door was closed behind her, she raced down the hallway and up the stairs to her bedchamber. She flung herself across the bed and pressed her fingers to lips that still tingled from his ravishment. She had always believed that Christmas was a time for miracles, but at that precise moment she wasn't certain exactly what she wished for.

CHAPTER FOUR

When Meredith entered the breakfast dining room the following morning, her gaze immediately shot to Chetwyn. She didn't know why she noticed him first. The room was far from empty. Several round tables were filled with guests. He sat at one against the far wall, near a window that provided a view of the gloomy skies. Lady Anne and Lord Tristan were with him. It irritated her that Chetwyn looked as though he'd slept well after their parting, while she'd done little more than toss and turn.

After going to the sideboard and selecting a few sumptuous items for her plate, she turned and spotted Litton sitting in a corner alone. Contriteness snapped at her because she hadn't noticed him sooner. She strolled over. "Good morning."

He looked up at her with bloodshot eyes. "Don't know what's so good about it."

His being out of sorts was unusual for him, or at least she thought it was. She realized that courting was a strange ritual in which one always saw others only at their best for a few hours, never for any great length of time. "The storm's let up, for one thing," she said, as a footman pulled out her chair and assisted her into it. With a flick of her wrist, she settled her napkin on her lap. She realized he smelled of stale cigars and old whiskey. "I was disappointed not to have a final dance with you last night."

With a low groan, he slammed his eyes closed. "I'm sorry, sweetheart. I was in the midst of a game of cards and lost track of the time."

"Were you winning?"

"No, luck wasn't with me." He twisted his lips into a sardonic grin. "To be honest, you're the only lucky thing to happen in my life of late."

"Lucky that we got caught in the garden, you mean?"

He gave her one of the smiles that had charmed her so many months earlier. "Simply lucky."

She sliced off a bit of sausage. "I don't suppose you told anyone about our encounter in the garden."

He appeared as flummoxed as she had been last night when Chetwyn had mentioned it. "Why would you think that?"

"It's just that there appears to be gossip going around about us and a kiss in the garden. As my father forbade my brothers to say anything—and they are quite familiar with his temper—I can't imagine how the rumors might have started."

"What does it matter? We're to be married in a little over a week."

"Yes, but we wanted people to believe that we were marrying because we wanted to, not because we were forced to as a result of my disgraceful behavior. My father is quite adamant that there be no scandal associated with our family."

Reaching across the table, he placed his hand over hers, where it rested beside her plate. "Be assured, my sweet, that I am marrying you because I *want* to. Scandal or no."

"Still, it's perplexing."

"People are always talking about one thing or another. Don't concern yourself with it."

"Yes, I suppose you're right." Although without the discovery in the garden, would she be marrying him? Choice had been taken away from her. It hadn't really mattered at the time because she liked Litton, and Chetwyn was involved with Lady Anne. But what if he hadn't been? What might have been was of no consequence. She would go mad if she focused on that rather than what was.

Shifting her gaze over to Chetwyn, she discovered him watching her. He would be about all day. Their paths might cross on occasion. Tonight a theater group would be performing *A Christmas Carol*, but until then she could find herself partnered with Chetwyn during a session of parlor games this afternoon. She could barely tolerate the thought.

"I was thinking of taking a walk," she told Litton.

"Where?"

She laughed lightly. "Outside, of course."

"My sweet, there's half a foot of snow out there."

"I have my boots. I thought you might care to join me."

Shaking his head, he rubbed his temples. "I feel as though my skull is about to split open."

"I'm so sorry. Why ever did you get out of bed, then?"

"I've not yet been to bed. I thought some coffee might help with the pounding in my head."

"You've been up all night?" She kept her horror at the

thought contained. What if he'd decided that he wanted a game of billiards, if he and other gentlemen had walked in to see Chetwyn kissing her—or worse, her returning the kiss with equal fervor? The scandal would have ruined her, perhaps even her family. Her father would have never forgiven her.

"Cards do not run on a schedule, so yes, all night," he said.

"But you were losing. Why would you keep at it?"

He shrugged. "I didn't wager that much."

While he didn't say it, she couldn't help but think that her dowry, which would soon be his, would settle his debt.

"Besides," he continued, "I can't expect you to understand the thrill of acquiring the perfect hand."

"You won't continue to gamble like this when we're married, will you?"

He stood. "I'm off to bed." Leaning down, he pressed a kiss to the top of her head. "I'll see you this evening."

When she glanced over and saw Chetwyn still studying her, she wished Litton had taken her in his arms and given her a resounding kiss that would cause the windows to fog over. She also wished that she wasn't suddenly filled with misgivings.

Chetwyn was standing outside taking in some fresh air when he spied Merry traipsing off in the direction of the castle that had once been the official family residence. He hadn't meant to stare at her during breakfast, but he'd had a rough night of it, unable to forget the feel of her in his arms. Watching her with Litton—touching, talking, and smiling—had been torment. He wanted to begin his day with her at *his* breakfast table.

Bloody hell. He wanted to begin his day with her in his bed. Breakfast would come later.

As she disappeared, he glanced around. Surely she wasn't going off by herself. She must have arranged a meeting with Litton, but then where was he? He knew she probably wouldn't welcome his company, but if he just happened to be strolling in the same direction—where was the harm? How could she object?

With the thick blanket of snow muffling his footsteps, Chetwyn took off after her. He remembered how much she enjoyed the outdoors. Perhaps like him, she was simply starting to feel hemmed in. The last thing he wanted was to play a game of charades, and he seemed to recall that was first on the list of today's entertainments. As he quickened his pace, he closed the distance between them and caught glimpses of her through the trees. She trudged on with such determination and purpose. In one gloved hand, she held a pair of skates, and he realized she was hoping to find a pond frozen over. He waited until she'd gone far enough that he didn't think she'd contemplate returning to the residence in order to avoid his company. Then he lengthened his stride until he caught up to her.

"Bit brisk out for a walk, isn't it?"

She swung around, the fire of anger in her eyes, when he much preferred the fire of passion. He was surprised that all of the snow around them didn't melt. "Let me be, Chetwyn."

"You can't possibly think that I'm going to allow you to march off into the woods alone."

"I'm certain I'll be quite safe."

It wasn't a risk he was willing to take. "Why isn't Litton accompanying you? Did you have a squabble during breakfast?"

"It's none of your affair." She pursed her lips before blurting, "His head hurt. He was up for a good bit of the night."

Drinking and gambling, he thought, based upon what he'd heard. Tristan had told Chetwyn over their warm eggs and toast that Litton had ended his night with markers owed to several of the lords. He didn't know why he wanted her to feel better about the blighter. "Many were, from what I understand."

"We're just fortunate that they didn't walk into the billiards room during an inopportune moment."

"I wouldn't have allowed your reputation to be sullied."

"Sometimes it can't be helped. Please return to the manor, Chetwyn. I'm out here alone because I need solitude."

"Are you rethinking your plans to marry Litton?"

"I'm rethinking my decision not to knock my skates against your thick skull."

He couldn't help but smile. "At least you are thinking of me."

"Good God, but you are vexing," she stated before tromping off.

He should let her go. She didn't want his company. But he might never have another opportunity to be in her presence alone. He looked up at the sky. Gray, with heavy clouds, it had an ominous feel to it.

Falling into step beside her, he said, "I think we're in for some more nasty weather."

"I'm quite capable of dealing with a bit of snow."

Holding his thoughts, he simply watched her breaths turning white and fading away. Her cheeks were ruddy, her strides determined. He remembered his father telling him about a well-stocked pond on the estate where he'd fished with the previous Duke of Keswick. Chetwyn wondered if that was where she was heading. She certainly seemed to know where she was going. She also seemed to have given up on attempting to convince him to leave her alone.

The bare trees were laden with snow. Every now and then a stray breeze blew a dusting of white from its perch. A hushed silence surrounded them. It seemed the place to let anger go, or at the very least a place to share a special moment, to create a memory that would last a lifetime. If he could not have her forever, he could at least have her for now. He didn't know if it would soften or sharpen the regret with which he would live.

He took her elbow. She pivoted around, her arm swinging the skates toward his head. He ducked, and when they'd passed he grabbed her other arm and propelled her back against the nearest tree; then, releasing the hold on one arm, he touched his finger to her lips, striving not to give any reaction to how warm they were. Despite the cold, the heat seeped through his leather gloves. "Shh."

"How dare—"

"Shh. We're not alone."

Her green eyes widened. The leaves would match their shade come spring. He would never behold another tree without thinking of her.

Without panic, barely moving her head, she scanned the area. "Who?"

"To your right, below that scraggly bush there."

She looked down. He saw her expression soften, before she shored up her resolve not to enjoy a moment in his company and gave him a pointed glare. "A rabbit?"

He'd spotted the white fur just before he touched Merry. "A tad beyond is a deer."

She shifted her gaze and he took satisfaction in her curiosity. "I remember the interest you took in birds when we walked through the parks. You seem to know them all."

"I appreciate creatures, great and small. What I do not appreciate is your taking liberties. Please unhand me."

"Do you love him? You never truly answered my question last night. Tell me that much at least. Do you love him?"

She angled her chin. "With all my heart."

Hope soaring through him, he gave her a slow, triumphant grin. "You always were a poor liar, Merry."

Then he covered her mouth with his.

Meredith knew that she should knock her skates against the side of his skull, render him unconscious, and run for her life. Instead she released her hold on them and wound her arms around his neck. As he moved in, she welcomed the weight and warmth of his body pressing against her.

It was wrong, so very wrong for her to enjoy his kiss, to want his kiss. Without liquor flavoring his tongue, he still tasted marvelous. Rich and sinful. Decadent. His gloved hands came up, held her head, provided a cushion against the hard bark. He took the kiss deeper, his tongue swirling through her mouth, stirring carnal cravings to life.

There had been a time when she'd thought she'd die from wanting a kiss from him. She never felt that way with Litton. When he had kissed her, his lips upon hers had been pleasant. But she'd never thought that together they could melt snow.

With Chetwyn, she was fairly certain that when he was done with her, she would find herself in a puddle of icy water. She stroked her hands over his shoulders. He was firm, strong. She knew he enjoyed the outdoors as much as she. His body reflected his passions. At one time, she'd hoped to become one of them.

He slid his lips from hers, nuzzling her neck, his mouth somehow finding its way beneath her collar, the heat of his breath coating dew along her skin. "Until Christmas, Merry, give me until Christmas to prove my affections are true."

Everything within her wanted to scream, "Yes!" But her heart, still bruised, whispered, "No."

"I'm afraid," she said, her voice as rough and raw as her soul.

Drawing back, he held her gaze, his rapid breaths visible in the cold air mingling with hers. "I won't hurt you again, I swear it."

He took her wrist. She wanted to wrench it free, but instead she was mesmerized watching as he brought it to his lips, crooked a finger beneath her cuff, and revealed a tiny bit of flesh. Gently, reverently, he placed his mouth there and closed his eyes as though he'd acquired heaven. Her breath caught, even as her heart sped into a wild gallop.

"Until Christmas, Merry," he whispered in a hoarse voice. "It's not so very long, and I'm a much better choice than Litton."

He opened his eyes, and the intensity she saw there almost dropped her to her knees. "It's too late, Chetwyn."

"Even if you were standing at the altar this moment, it wouldn't be too late. It's not too late until you exchange vows, until you sign the marriage register."

Shaking her head, she pushed him back and skirted away from him. She tugged down her cuff, yanked up her glove, but still she could feel the press of his lips against her wrist. She wanted to rub the sensation away, while at the same time she wanted to place it in a gilded box so she could keep it. "I trusted you with my heart once. I won't do it again."

"I know I bruised your feelings."

"You did nothing of the sort." Reaching down, she snatched up her skates.

"I won't give up," he said. "Not until Christmas."

"Why that particular day?"

"Because your love is the only gift I wish to receive."

Oh, how she truly wanted to believe the words, to bask in them, glory in them. But he had toyed with her affections once. She would not be so quick to fall for him again. "And with my love comes my dowry. How do I know it's not what you're truly after?"

"I don't give a damn about your dowry. I'll find a way to prove that to you as well."

"Even if you earn my love, you won't win my hand. Father promised it to Litton."

He narrowed his eyes. "Was it not your choice to marry him? Are the rumors true? Did he take advantage?"

"It was only a kiss, but we were caught. I wanted the kiss, and I want to marry him." Or at least she had convinced herself that she wanted to marry him, because in truth she had no choice. Her father would have it no other way. She wondered if a time would ever come when women didn't have to obey their fathers, when they would have the full freedom of adulthood. Although even her brothers, older than she, still obeyed their father. "The pond is just over the rise," she said, to steer them away from the conversation and a promise she didn't want to make.

She and Chetwyn carried on in companionable silence as the sky darkened and snow began to blow around them.

"Perhaps we should turn back," he said.

"Giving up so easily, Chetwyn?"

"Where you're concerned, never again."

She didn't want to admit that, with his words, something within her sang as clearly as the birds of spring.

The snow was falling more thickly by the time they reached the pond.

"I wouldn't recommend we stay overly long," Chetwyn said. "Our tracks will soon disappear, and we'll have a difficult time finding our way back."

Something told her that they shouldn't stay at all. They'd walked quite a distance. The wind had picked up and was whining through the trees. Soon it would be howling. But the water was frozen and the ice inviting. "One trip around the outer edge, and we'll head back," she said.

She glanced around, striving to determine where she could sit without gaining a damp bottom.

"Lean against that tree there," he said. "I'll slip your blades onto your shoes."

After handing him her blades, she did as he suggested. With her back against the bark, she watched as he knelt in the snow. He lifted his gaze to hers, and a sharp pang ripped through her. She had dreamed of him in that position, only he was going to ask her to become his wife. She swallowed hard at the memory of how badly she had wanted it.

Chetwyn patted his knee. "Give me your foot."

With her hands to the side, gripping the trunk of the tree, she lifted her foot. Bending his head, he went to work securing the wooden blade to her shoe. Give him until Christmas to prove he was worthy of her affections? She didn't think he'd need more than a day. What of poor Litton? She knew what it was to be cast aside. He certainly didn't deserve such unkind treatment, but was it kinder to let him go when she longed for another?

When Chetwyn finished with one foot, she placed the other on his knee.

"A pity you didn't bring blades," she told him.

"I shall walk along beside you."

"On the ice?"

"On the bank."

"I shan't be able to skate very far."

He set her other foot aside and unfolded that long, lean body of his. "As you don't know how thick the ice is, you're better off staying close to shore, where the water is shallow. If you break through the ice, you'll only get your feet wet."

"I'm familiar with the dangers of ice skating. I've never had ice buckle beneath me."

"Then let's not have today be the first time."

She didn't think it would be. It was so terribly cold up

here. If she didn't spend a good deal of her time outdoors, she'd no doubt be shivering. But her woolen riding habit and heavy cloak helped to keep her somewhat warm. Having Chetwyn nearby didn't hurt either.

With her hand on his arm, she cut a swathe through the snow until they reached the pond. It was strange, but the blue of the water viewed through the ice reminded her of the eyes of the Pembrook lords.

"Do you suppose it's possible that Keswick's ancestors studied this pond in winter for so long that it changed the shade of their eyes?" she asked.

"Are you trying to weave a fairy tale?"

"I guess I am being fanciful. I tend to do that from time to time. It's only that they have such unusual eyes."

"Not boring like mine."

She jerked her head around to stare at him. "They're not boring." They were the color of hot cocoa when there was more cocoa than milk. And they spoke volumes, which was the reason that she'd thought he would be asking for her hand. She had read so much into his words based upon what his eyes were saying. Now she was afraid to read too much, to believe that the affection she saw there was true.

He led her onto the ice. While he may have wished to walk alongside her, she glided much faster than he walked. She slipped her hand away from his.

"Don't go out far, Merry."

"Honestly, Chetwyn, you worry too much. The duchess told me that the pond has been iced over for a couple of weeks now."

"That doesn't mean it's perfectly safe."

Safer than you, she thought. She welcomed the brisk air brushing over her face, the snow melting on her eyelashes. With the silence, she could almost imagine that she was completely and absolutely alone. It was what she'd thought she wanted.

Only now she realized that she wanted to be with him: walking, talking, her arm linked with his. She pirouetted to face him. She heard a crack of thunder. He was rushing toward her.

"Merry, don't move!"

Another crack, louder than the first, and she realized with horror that the storm wasn't above her, but beneath her.

"Chetwyn!"

Then the ice gave way.

CHAPTER FIVE

Chetwyn managed to grab her and haul her to the bank with enough force that they both tumbled onto the snow. Fortunately, not enough of the ice had given way that she was in danger of falling through, but still his heart was pounding. "Are you all right?" he asked.

She nodded, then released a breath that was more laugh than air. "I was terrified for a moment there. It sounded awful. I'm embarrassed that I screamed."

"I barely heard it because of my shout. But I think we should head back now."

"Yes, indeed. The weather seems to be worsening at an amazing clip."

The snowfall was heavier, damp and sticky. The wind was circling around in gales. He removed her skates, then shoved himself to his feet before pulling her up. He entwined his arm with hers, faced in the direction from which they'd come, and realized that a good bit of the visibility was lost to them. "Stay close," he ordered, and he felt her hold on him tighten.

They walked as quickly as possible, which wasn't fast

enough, as far as he was concerned. Her strides were shorter than his, and she was having a difficult time keeping up. He could feel her trembling as the wind howled around them and the snow fell in a constant wash of thick, heavy flakes. Barely breaking his stride, he shrugged out of his coat and draped it over her shoulders.

"Chetwyn, it's too cold."

"I'll be fine," he lied as the wind sliced through him.

Why had he not insisted that they head back? He had wanted more time with her, to speak with her, to try to make his case.

How far had they walked? Had he taken a wrong turn? It was as he'd anticipated. The snow had begun filling in their tracks, and he could no longer be sure they were on the right path. Tiny shards of ice sliced at him. Where the devil were they?

Looking around, striving to get his bearings, he saw the crenellated outline of Pembrook Castle, the original holding. The recently built manor would be on the other side, up a rise that he didn't know if she'd have the strength to climb. He could carry her, but even then it was so far. If he stumbled, what would become of her? It didn't bare thinking about. He wasn't going to let anything happen to her.

"We'll take refuge in the old castle," he said.

"No, I don't want to go there."

"Merry, we don't have much choice. The manor is still a good distance away."

"I didn't realize we'd gone so far."

"My charms distracted you."

She laughed. It was so good to hear her laugh. "How can you be pompous at a time like this?"

Because he needed to distract her again, to give her something to focus on other than their dire circumstances. He pushed them forward, slogging through the drifts of snow. How could such a fierce storm have come upon them so quickly? He was more familiar with the weather in the south, in Cornwall. He'd always heard that the north was brutal, but until now he hadn't understood what that meant.

By the time they reached the old manor and slumped against the stone wall, he realized it was madness to try to get her to the new residence. He had to get her dry and warm. "We've no choice. We're going to stop here."

"We can . . . carry on," she stammered, her teeth chattering with such force he was surprised they didn't crack.

"Perhaps we'll give it a try after we've warmed up and gathered our strength."

She didn't argue as they made their way along the side of the building. He fought the strong gale that wanted to smash him into it, into her. As much as possible, he was trying to shield her from the fury of nature. Finally, he saw a door. Reaching out, he closed his fingers over the handle, released the latch, and felt relief swamp him when it gave way.

Nearly torn from its hinges by the wind, the wooden door banged against the wall. He ushered her into the kitchen and staggered in after her. Closing the door, he took stock of their surroundings. Although the building had been abandoned, not everything had been taken. There was a stove, a table, a stack of wood. He didn't think it likely that he would find food, but for now it gave him hope that he had found a shelter from the storm.

"Come along, let's see what we've got."

With Merry in his wake, he stalked down a darkened hallway and then another, a bit of light coming through a window at the end guiding him. Then he walked into what had once been a great hall. The fireplace was massive, the sort where the master of the household might have roasted deer.

He knelt before it, grateful to find more wood, kindling, and matches. He set himself to the task of getting a fire going. It wasn't long before the flames were blazing, sending out welcomed warmth.

"Oh, th-that's l-lovely," she whispered as she moved closer to the fire.

Glancing around, he noticed the draperies. They would have to do. He rushed across the room, grabbed a handful of the fabric, and with a sharp tug, brought them down. Dust motes kicked up around him, but at least the curtains were dry.

He hurried back over to her and dropped them at her feet. "Take off your clothes."

Merry stared at him as though he'd gone mad. "I beg your pardon?"

"Yours are damp, mine are drenched. We have to get warm before I lose my senses, and you are truly alone. Body heat is the fastest way. You'll have some privacy while I see what else I can find. Wrap those draperies about you."

He made his way through a good portion of the residence, tearing down more moth-eaten draperies. He located a half-full bottle of rum.

Returning to the great room, he strove to ignore the pile of clothes near the fire and what that signified. Merry sat on the floor, the draperies pulled in close about her. He fashioned a crude pallet with what he'd found. Then he handed her the bottle of rum. "Drink this. It'll warm you."

Although not as much as I plan to. Turning away from her, he began removing his own clothes. He tore off his jacket, but his fingers were too stiff with the cold to loosen the buttons. He was going to have to rip—

"Here," she said, suddenly standing in front of him. The drapery was wrapped around her, gathered in front of her. With just a shrug of her shoulders, it would pool on the floor. "You drink now."

His fingers were so numb he thought he might drop the bottle, but he managed to hold on to it and take deep swallows. He was aware of her fingers working his buttons free.

"I've dreamed of you doing this," he said.

She jerked her gaze up to his, and he was surprised that his facial muscles were warm enough to grin.

"Remove my clothes," he explained in case his meaning wasn't clear. "I would have liked to have removed yours, but you seemed rather alarmed by the notion of what I was suggesting."

"It's scandalous. I was brought up to avoid scandal at all costs, and yet I seem to find myself slipping into the quagmire of it once again." She helped him out of his waistcoat, then slowly unraveled his neckcloth.

"How long do you think we'll be here?" she asked, and he heard the trepidation mirrored in her voice.

"Only until the storm passes."

"That could be days."

"Could be years."

She grinned at him. He was grateful for that. "I don't know where I'd be now if you hadn't gone on the walk with me."

"I doubt you'd have stayed out as long if I hadn't been serving as a distraction."

"Probably not." She peeled his shirt up over his head. He welcomed the warmth from the fire finally dancing over his skin.

"You're like ice," she said.

"Unfortunately."

"Can you manage your trousers?"

"If I must."

She laughed lightly. "Yes, in this instance I think you must."

Moving away, she sat on the mound of draperies, her back to him. He wasn't as cold or shaking as he had been. They probably no longer needed the warmth of each other's bodies. The fire would suffice. But it seemed a shame to waste the opportunity of having her so near when it might never come again.

Beyond the glass and stone, it sounded as though demons trapped in hell howled.

"It's only the wind, Merry."

They were enclosed in a cocoon of warmth provided by the ragged draperies. Their clothes were resting near the fire. They appeared to be somewhat dry. She should probably gather up her things and get dressed, but she didn't want to move. She thought she might like to stay here forever.

"I've heard this manor is haunted."

"Is that why you hesitated to stop here?"

She nodded. "I know it's silly to believe in ghosts, but there you are."

"Nothing about you is silly."

She couldn't deny the pleasure his words brought. "They'll have noticed I'm missing by now—have noticed we both are, no doubt."

"They won't come looking yet. Their visibility is no better than ours."

"When my father finds us here, he'll insist that we marry. Being alone with a gentleman in an abandoned manor during a storm is more scandalous than being discovered in a man's arms near a trellis of roses in a dark corner of the garden."

With his finger trailing along her neck, he slid her hair over her shoulder and pressed his lips to her nape. In spite of their warmth, she shivered. "But does he hold your heart? You captured mine from the beginning."

Twisting around, she looked sharply at him. "Then why did you give your attentions to Lady Anne?"

Cradling her face with one hand, he stroked his thumb along her cheek. "Out of a misguided notion that I owed it to my brother." He held her gaze, and she found herself swimming in the depths of his brown eyes. "He wrote me a letter as he was dying and asked me to see to her happiness."

"But he died long before you gave me any attention."

"Unfortunately, the officer who had the letter did not deliver it until this past spring. He feared it getting lost, and so he brought it himself. If not for me, Walter would not be dead."

Her heart went out to him at the fissure of guilt that ran through his voice with his words. "You did not make him ill."

"No, but he'd have not been there had I possessed the funds for him to live like a gentleman. The income from my estates is dwindling. I couldn't support him in the manner in which he wished to live, so we agreed that a commission in the army was best. Not an hour passes by that I don't miss him, not a day goes by that I don't regret not finding another way. I could have married any number of women with dowries that would have provided me with the means to live more luxuriously. Instead, I was holding out for love. I was waiting for you."

She did not move away when his lips joined hers. His tongue stroked the seam of her mouth, urging her to open it for him. She shouldn't have, but she did, because if she was honest with herself, she would admit that she had been waiting for him as well. She'd had offers for marriage during her first Season, but she'd turned them all away, had thought perhaps she would be more content as a spinster. Until the ball when she spied him across the room, that is. When their eyes had met, it was as though he were standing right in front of her, touching her, gazing into her soul, weaving some sort of spell over her. When he'd asked her to dance, she'd thought she'd arrived in heaven.

Then this Season when he'd informed her that he would be pursuing Lady Anne, she'd wondered what she had done to douse the passion that had trembled on the edge between them.

Yet here it was again, blazing to life.

She twisted around completely, giving him easier access to her mouth, and with a deep growl he deepened the kiss, threading the fingers of one hand through the tangled mess of her hair and holding her in place, while the other hand stroked her back, squeezed a shoulder, skimmed down her side, and came around to cup her breast.

She knew she should be incensed with the liberties he was taking. Instead, she moaned softly and took both her hands over a similar journey, noting the corded muscles of his back, the flatness of his stomach, the breadth of his chest. Smooth. Silk over steel. It was as though he'd been forged by the gods. His clothing hid well his attributes, and she felt as though she were discovering little buried treasures.

Dragging his mouth along the arch of her throat, he rasped, "I want you, Merry. You can't imagine how much I want you."

Oh, she could imagine it very well, because she wanted him. As wrong as it was, she wanted him with an intensity that fairly threatened to destroy her. When Litton had kissed her in the garden, she hadn't wanted to melt into him, to meld her body with his. With Chetwyn, all rational thought scattered away like dried leaves before an autumn breeze. She couldn't think, didn't want to think, wanted only to feel the eager press of his hands, the hunger of his mouth against her flesh.

Shifting his weight, he carried her down to their makeshift velveteen bed. She thought the thickest of mattresses could not be more welcoming. Rising above her, he stared down on her. She combed her fingers through his unruly locks before bringing her palms down to cradle his jaw. The rough bristles tickled her tender skin.

"I was a fool, Merry," he whispered. "Misguided, trying to do right by my brother, putting my own wants, needs, and happiness aside. I want you. I *need* you. You bring me happiness such as I've never known. Let me show you how much I can love you."

She swallowed hard. She knew he wasn't speaking of flowers or poetry or chocolates. He wanted to give of himself, completely and absolutely. He wanted her to freely accept what he was offering. When they were discovered here, the scandal would be insurmountable. Alone with him through the storm. Litton would let her go. Her father would insist Chetwyn marry her. She would be ruined. She might as well be ruined in truth.

Besides, she desired him with a fervor that she thought would be her undoing. If she didn't have him at that moment, she would probably die anyway. Reaching up, she placed her hand on the nape of his neck and brought him down.

He latched his mouth onto hers with a fierceness that matched the storm. Hot, heavy, and passionate as though walls existed that needed to be torn down. He made short work of removing the covers that separated them, and then they were bare flesh against bare flesh from top to toe. Velvety warmth that could have melted the thickest pond surrounded them. She felt her heart's resistance giving way inch by inch as his hands and fingers explored her, while hers did the same with him. Broad shoulders, strong back, taut buttocks.

He had rescued her from the pond, guided her through the storm, and created a haven for them to wait out the screeching winds. He had managed to hold her fears at bay, and she'd known that somehow he would save her.

A small part of her wondered if he was saving her now as well.

She couldn't marry Litton after this. She wouldn't marry him. One night he had pursued her with purpose. But once her hand and dowry were secured, passion, desire, whatever it was that had led them into the garden had taken refuge, never to be seen again. With Chetwyn, it always hovered near the surface, threatened to join them, promised to carry them to exalted heights.

Here she was, clamoring up those heights, unafraid as Chetwyn's mouth trailed over every inch of her, exploring, enticing, kissing provocatively. The bend of her elbow, the back of her knee, the turn of her ankle, the tip of her tiny toe. Down, up, over, and around. He left no part of her untouched.

His mouth returned to hers as he nestled himself between her thighs. She felt the pressure of him, the weight, the heat. She lifted her hips to receive him. Holding back her cry at the sharp pain as he sank fully into her, she concentrated on his mouth, its texture, its flavor. She focused on his hair, the strands that were never tamed for long.

His movements were slow, leisurely. The pain eased, and pleasure slipped in to replace it, sweet and ripe, like a new bud feeling the sun coaxing it up. With each petal unfurled, the pleasure increased. Thrashing her head from side to side, she anchored herself to him as he took her on a journey for which there were no words.

She cried out as the release slammed into her, as her world darkened, then exploded into light. With a rough groan, he gave a final thrust and stilled, his arms closing more tightly around her. Lethargy worked its way through her.

The last thing she heard was his whispered, "I love you," before sleep claimed her.

Chapter Six

It was the baying of the hounds that woke her. Nestled against Chetwyn beneath the draperies, her cheek against his chest, she became acutely aware of his stiffening.

"It's morning. The storm's passed," he said before throwing back the covering and coming to his feet.

In fascination, she watched his bare backside as he strode to the window. The light from the dying fire was enough to give her an impressive view. He was quite marvelously carved of flesh, muscle, sinew, and bone.

"A search party," he continued before turning about and heading back toward her.

Did it make her a wanton because she couldn't help but smile at the sight of him?

"Is my father among them?" she asked.

"Afraid so. Your brothers, too, from the looks of it. Litton and both Pembrook lords."

After gathering up his clothes, he knelt beside her and cradled her face. "Tell them you made your way here, but the storm prevented you from going farther, and you've been waiting it out."

"I don't understand. You'll be here."

He stroked her cheek, and the sadness in his eyes almost made her weep. "No. I won't have your reputation dragged through the mud by having us found together."

She flattened her hand against his chest. "But the discovery of us together will ensure that we marry. My father will very well insist."

He brought her in close, then tucked her beneath his chin. "I want you, Merry, more than I've ever wanted anything in my life, but not at the risk of bringing you shame or more pain than I've already caused. Nor will I do as Litton and force you into marriage." Dipping his head, he kissed her short and sweet, but in the tenderness of the moment she heard volumes: love, caring, goodbye.

Then he was rushing out of the room as though the hounds of hell were nipping at his heels, while the duke's hounds were barking more loudly with their approaching nearness. Feeling lost and bereft, she went through the motions of slipping back into her stiff but dried riding habit. She was buttoning up the last of the pearl disks when she heard a door slam open and the stomp of feet.

Her father was the first to come barging through the doorway. "Meredith, thank God. What in the blazes happened, girl?"

"I . . . I got caught in the storm. I wanted to go ice skating."

Litton approached and swept his coat around her. "You must have been terrified."

"Only of the ghosts. I've heard the manor is haunted."

"The tower and the dungeon," the duke said, studying her carefully. "Not the manor itself."

"Well, then, I had nothing to fear."

"I don't suppose you've seen Lord Chetwyn," Lord Tristan asked. "We've not been able to find him."

Her mouth dry, she shook her head. "No, our paths didn't cross, but I'm certain he's all right. He probably just went for a walk. But he's familiar enough with the outdoors that he would have taken shelter."

Litton placed his arm around her shoulders. "Come, we must get you back to the residence. You must be famished."

"Quite."

She allowed him to lead her from the room but she couldn't help glancing back over her shoulder. Lord Tristan had a speculative gleam in his eyes as he studied the mound of draperies. He had a reputation for being quite the rogue, and she hoped he couldn't guess what had truly transpired here.

From the master's bedchamber upstairs, Chetwyn watched as the search party headed back toward the manor. For a few hours, he held in his arms every dream he'd ever dreamed, and once again he'd let her go.

To have her, he would have to ruin her, and he loved her far too much for that. But neither could he bear the thought of her with Litton.

"Thought I'd find you somewhere about."

He spun around at the sound of Lord Tristan's voice.

"Trying to protect the lady's reputation?" Lord Tristan asked.

Chetwyn sighed. "I seem to recall your doing a very similar thing for Anne."

"And it almost cost me a life of happiness."

"I could never be happy if Meredith suffered because of scandal."

Lord Tristan ambled over, leaned against the window casing, and looked out. "Suppose I could say that I found you in the tower."

Chetwyn shook his head. "Too close."

"The abbey ruins then. We shall have to wait here for an hour or so to make that believable."

With a nod, Chetwyn pressed his back to the wall and slid down to the floor. He glanced up as Tristan offered him a silver flask. He said nothing as he took it and drank deeply. Rum. It might warm the coldness that had settled in his chest when he'd watched Meredith walk away without looking back.

LORRAINE HEATH

CHAPTER SEVEN

Meredith awoke in a fog. She remembered the warm bath, the tray of food, and the bed covers slipped over her. She'd fought off sleep, wanting to wait until Chetwyn returned, but exhaustion had claimed her. Rolling onto her side, she stared at the burgundy draperies, thinking of others that she'd recently encountered. They were drawn aside, and through the windowpane she could see the darkness. She'd slept through the day. They'd missed the play. Tonight was the ball. She needed to get dressed and see how Chetwyn was. She knew Lord Tristan had stayed behind to continue searching for him. She wondered if he'd found him or if Chetwyn had made his own way here.

Reaching over, she yanked on her bell pull to summon the maid who had been assigned to her. When the door opened, however, it was Lady Anne who walked through.

"Oh, finally, you're awake."

"Lord Chetwyn?"

"Doing remarkably well. Tristan announced that he found him at the abbey ruins, although I shall eat my favorite bonnet if Tristan truly found him there and not at the castle."

Meredith felt the heat suffuse her face. While she didn't know Lady Anne well, they shared a common interest: Chetwyn. Meredith felt as though she could trust her with anything involving him. "He didn't want us to be found together."

"No, he wouldn't have, now, would he?"

"Why do you say that?"

"Because I know him well enough to know that he would give to you what he once gave to me."

With her brow furrowed, Meredith stared at her. "What was that?"

"The gift of choice."

As Meredith descended the stairs, she could hear the orchestra playing a quadrille, the first dance of the night, according to the dance card that the duchess had given her. She much preferred the waltz. She considered going to the grand salon. Instead, she turned into the parlor and walked over to the small decorated tree that sat on a table near a window. Tiny boxes were gathered beneath the boughs. Meredith had little doubt that they contained treats that the duchess would pass out to her guests tomorrow upon their parting. She would return home to spend the holiday with her family, and a few days afterward she would be moving into the residence she would share with Litton. Where she would share his bed. Where he would touch her and kiss her and bring her pleasure, and she would do the same with him.

And all the while she would think of Chetwyn, who could have stayed by her side this morning. Then she would be marrying him. In the years to come, would each have wondered if the person sitting across the table was the one they would have chosen—if given a choice?

Only she had a choice. Chetwyn had ensured it by leaving.

"Oh, there you are. I'd heard you were finally up and about."

Turning slightly, she smiled at Litton. "Yes, I had quite the lovely nap."

"Let's go have our dance, shall we?"

"How many?" she asked.

"Pardon?"

"How many dances?"

"Well, two, of course. The first and the last."

"And in between?"

"You shall dance with others, and I shall play cards."

Four dances the night they met. She wondered how long it would be before he desired only one . . . and then none.

She swallowed hard, considering if she really wanted to know the truth, but she had to put the niggling doubts to rest. "The night when we were discovered kissing in the garden, during Greystone's ball—I heard my father and brothers coming."

He stared at her as though she'd lost her senses. "As did I."

"I tried to slip away, so we wouldn't be caught. You held me tight and whispered that it would be all right."

He smiled. "And it did turn out all right, didn't it?"

"Would you have held me so tightly if I had no dowry?"

He laughed. "Now you're being silly. Let's go join the merriment."

He took her arm, and she shook him off. "I'm serious, Litton. We had time *not* to get caught."

"I wanted to marry you," he said impatiently. "Is that suddenly a crime?"

"Not a crime, but not entirely right, either." She thought of the kiss that Chetwyn had bestowed upon her in the billiards room. Then again when they were walking. At the castle. It was as though he couldn't get enough of her, would never have enough of her. "Do you know that we have not kissed once since that night? Not once."

"I took liberties that night I should not have taken. I've been trying to spare you any further gossip."

She narrowed her eyes. "So you did tell people about the kiss in the garden."

He shrugged. "Only as a precaution."

"Against what?"

"Your father changing his mind and thinking that it didn't matter, that our marriage was not in order."

She gave a light laugh. "Since he's withdrawn the dowry, that's not likely to happen, as he knows no one else will have me now."

He grabbed her arms, jerked her. "What are you talking about?"

Not a lie, she told herself, but a small test. "My father has decided, based upon the recent worry I caused him, that I shall not come with a dowry."

Releasing her, he plowed his hands through his hair. "I won't have it. We discussed the settlement. Granted, we haven't signed the papers, but I was depending on that dowry to cover my gaming debts. I shall have a word—"

"Don't bother," she said. "I shan't be marrying you, with or without the dowry."

He narrowed his eyes. "Have you been testing me? You silly girl, I'll tell everyone what happened in the garden. Your reputation will be ruined. No one will have you."

"I think you may be wrong on that score." At least she hoped he was. But even if he wasn't, as she walked from the room, she realized that she'd been spared making a grave mistake.

"—twenty stitches per inch."

Chetwyn tried to look impressed with his present dance partner's sewing skills, but the truth was that Lady Beatrix's words merely collided together as they bombarded his ears and made no sense. He'd heard that Merry had recovered from her ordeal and would be coming to the ballroom before the night was done, so he was trying to distract himself. A part of him wished desperately that he had stayed by her side at the castle. It would have ensured she became his wife.

But he didn't want her forced into something she might not want. He just didn't know where he would find the strength to stay away from her once she married Litton. But stay away he would, because the last thing he wanted was her unhappiness.

"Pardon me."

At the tap on his shoulder, he came to an abrupt halt and almost forgot to breathe. Merry stood there in a striking red velvet dress with white trim. She smiled at him, and this time his heart nearly forgot to beat. Then she turned her attention to Lady Beatrix.

"Forgive me for interrupting, but a gentleman asked me to give this to you," she said, holding out a slip of paper.

"Oh." Lady Beatrix took it, unfolded it, and read it. She blinked her eyes. "Who gave this to you?"

"He asked me not to say. He wanted to remain a bit mysterious, I think. But I am given to understand that he is quite impressed with your sewing skills."

Lady Beatrix brightened. "Indeed. I knew some gentleman would eventually appreciate them." She looked at Chetwyn. "If you will excuse me, my lord, I must see to this."

"By all means. Who am I to stand in the way of true love?"

Lady Beatrix gave a tiny squeal before hurrying from the room.

Chetwyn studied Meredith. "What have you done, Merry?"

"I wanted to dance with you."

"Well, then, allow me the honor."

Taking her in his arms, he swept her over the dance floor. "Who was the note from?"

She smiled. "Me, of course. It said only, 'Meet me in the library.'"

"At least she'll be warm."

Her smile grew. "And not alone. I saw Lord Wexford going in there on my way here."

He laughed. "Jolly good."

She blushed. "Who knows? Perhaps something will come of it."

Tightening his hold on her, he asked, "And what of us? Will anything come of us?"

"I'm not quite sure. It depends on you, I suppose. You should know that within my pocket I have a slip of paper for every lady you intend to dance with tonight. I want all of your dances."

"You shall have them."

"You should also be aware that Father threatened to take away my dowry if I didn't marry Litton. I suppose he knew I had reservations and thought to dispense with them. I don't know if he'll carry through on his threat."

"I've told you before that I don't give a damn about your dowry."

She took a deep breath. "I don't love Litton. I never did, but he seemed a pleasant enough sort, and he made me feel appreciated. I thought I would be content with him, but then I discovered something I wanted more. Just a few moments ago, I cried off with him. He plans to tell everyone about the tryst in the garden. I shall be ruined."

"Lovely chap. I shall introduce him to my fist later. But right this moment you do know that the best way to stop gossip is to give people something far more interesting to talk about."

She nodded. "I never stopped loving you."

His heart contracted, then expanded, and he thought it might burst through his chest. "That's good, because I have loved you from the night we met, and I shall love you until the day I die."

"Then kiss me now."

And he did. He stopped dancing, folded his arms around her, and lowered his mouth to hers. He heard the slowing of feet, a few gasps, some chuckles, a clap or two. Yes, they would be the talk of high society. But he wasn't quite done.

Breaking off the kiss, he held her warm gaze for but a moment before going down on bended knee and taking her hand.

All dancing halted. The music stopped.

"Merry, will you do me the honor of becoming my wife, my marchioness, the mother of my children? Will you be my love for as long as I draw breath?"

Tears welled in her eyes, as she pressed a trembling hand to her lips. "Oh, Chetwyn, yes, of course."

Taking from his pocket a ring with small emeralds that matched her eyes, he slipped it onto her finger. At her stunned expression, he couldn't help but smile. "I told you, Merry, that first night that you were the reason I was here. Happy Christmas, my love."

Standing, he kissed her again as a rousing cheer went up from those who surrounded them. As her arms closed around his neck, he pulled her in against the curve of his body and held her tighter. It was going to be a very lovely Christmas for them both. The first of many.

Read on for a thrilling peek at the final book in
the Lost Lords of Pembrook trilogy,

LORD OF WICKED INTENTIONS,

by *New York Times* bestseller Lorraine Heath
from Avon Books,
May 2013

An Excerpt from

LORD OF WICKED INTENTIONS

The invitation came because of a debt owed. Owed to him. All debts were owed to him, while he owed no man anything. Not his friendship, not his loyalty, not his kindness. And certainly not his hard-earned coin.

But the Earl of Wortham, a man of little *worth*, Rafe Easton thought snidely, did owe him a good deal of coin, which was the reason that he was allowed into the earl's magnificent library. He wondered briefly how long it would be before it was stripped of all the former owner's prized possessions. The late earl had left his son with little, and what remained had been quickly gambled away in Rafe's club.

The man wanted his credit extended, and so for tonight he pretended a friendship with the Rakehell Club's owner.

Drinking fine Scotch that the earl could scarce afford, Rafe lounged insolently in a chair near the fireplace while the other lords mingled about, chuckled, chatted, and downed far too much liquor. They were a randy lot. He could sense their eagerness and anticipation hovering thickly about the room.

The young earl had a sister, although he didn't recognize her as such. No, more precisely, she was the late earl's daughter, born on the wrong side of the blanket. But at his father's deathbed, Wortham had given his word that he would see to her care, and that was what tonight's gathering was about.

Finding someone willing to see to her care.

Wortham swore she was a virgin, and that knowledge had some of the lords salivating, while others had sent their excuses. Rafe didn't give a whit one way or the other. He did not bother with mistresses. They tended to cling, to desire baubles, to lead a man down a merry path only to eventually grow weary of the bed in which they slept and seek another.

He didn't do anything that even reeked of permanence because anything that hinted at forever could be snatched away, could leave him, *would* leave him. Even his gaming establishment—he took no pride in it. It was simply a means to coins in his pockets. It could be taken away, and he could walk from it without looking back, without a measure of regret. He had nothing in his life that meant anything at all to him, that would cause him the least hurt if he should lose it. His emotions ran on a perfected, even keel, and he liked it that way. Every decision he made was based on cold calculations.

He was here tonight to watch these lords make fools of themselves as they vied for the lady's attention, to measure their weaknesses, and to discover means of exploiting them.

He'd heard that his brothers had been invited. That was a waste of ink on paper. They were both married and so disgustingly devoted to their wives that he couldn't see either of them straying, not even an inch. But then, what did he truly know about his siblings?

They'd finally returned to England two years later than they'd promised, Tristan a few months earlier than Sebastian. Rafe's man had been waiting and ensured they made their way to the gaming hell. Rafe had greeted their arrival with little more than a glass of whiskey. He'd provided them with rooms and food until they'd secured Sebastian's place as duke. He'd seen little of them since.

His choice. They invited him to join them for dinners, for sailing, for Christmas. He declined. He didn't need them cluttering his life. He liked things exactly as they were. He was his own man, responsible to no one beyond himself.

From somewhere down a hallway, a clock began to chime the hour of nine. Conversations ceased. The lords stilled, their gazes riveted on the door. Sipping his Scotch, Rafe watched through half-lowered lids as the door opened. He caught sight of a purple hem and then—

He nearly choked on the golden liquid, as he fought not to give any reaction at all.

He suddenly had an acute understanding of why Adam was so quick to fall from grace when confronted with the temptation that was Eve. Wortham's sister was the most ex-quisite creature Rafe had ever seen. Her hair, a shade that rivaled the sun in brilliance, was piled up to reveal a long, graceful neck that sloped down to alabaster shoulders that begged for a man's lips to make their home there. She was neither short nor tall, but somewhere roughly in the middle. He wasn't exactly certain where her head might land against his body. The curve of his shoulder perhaps. She was not particularly voluptuous, but she contained an elegance that drew the eye and spoke of still waters that could very well drown a man if he were of a mind to go exploring within their depths.

Which he wasn't. He was content to appreciate the surface. It told him all he needed—all he desired—to know.

Glancing around, she appeared confused, her smile uncertain, until Wortham eventually crossed the room to stand beside her without looking, as though he was with her. Two people could hardly appear more different. Wortham stood stiff as a poker, while she was composed but emitted a softness. She would be the sort to touch, hold, and comfort. Rafe almost shuddered with the realization.

"Gentlemen, Miss Evelyn Chambers."

She dipped elegantly into a flawless curtsy. "My lords."

He'd expected her voice to be sweet, to match her smile, but it was smoky, rich, the song of decadence and wickedness. He imagined that voice in a lower pitch, whispering of naughty pleasures, curling around his ear, traveling through his blood. He imagined deep, throaty laughter and sultry eyes, lost to heated passion.

"Visit with the gentlemen," Wortham ordered.

Again, she gave the impression of one confused, but then she straightened her lovely shoulders and began making her way from one man to the next, a butterfly trying to determine upon which petal to light, which would be sturdy enough to support her in the manner to which she was accustomed.

He caught glimpses of her face as she worked the crowd of a dozen men. A shy smile here, a bolder one there. Furrowed brow when a gentleman rested a hand on her shoulder or arm. Fluttering eyelashes as she expertly glided beyond reach without offending. He wasn't quite certain she understood the rules of the game she was playing. Could she be that innocent?

Her mother had been the late earl's mistress. Surely she knew what her mother's role in his life had been—to warm his bed, to bring him pleasure, to keep him satisfied.

Sometimes she seemed to have confidence, to know exactly what she was doing. Other times she seemed baffled by the conversation. Still, it was as though she were ticking off a list, speaking to each man for only a moment or two before moving on, never returning to a man once they were acquainted.

Come to me, he thought. *Come to me*. Then he shoved the wayward thoughts aside. What did he care if she didn't notice him? He was accustomed to living in the shadows, to not being seen. The gossamer depths offered protection equal to the strongest armor. No one bothered him there unless he desired it.

He didn't desire her, yet he couldn't deny that he wondered what her skin might feel like against the tips of his fingers. Soft. Silky. Warm. It had been so very long since he'd been warm. Even the fire by which he sat now couldn't thaw his frigid core. He liked it that way, preferred it.

Nothing touched him, nothing bothered him. Nothing mattered.

She matters.

No, she didn't. She was an earl's by-blow on the verge of becoming some man's ornament. A very graceful ornament to be sure. An extremely lovely one. But she would be relegated to the same importance as a work of art: to be looked upon, to be touched, to bring pleasure when pleasure was sought.

She glanced around, appearing to be lost within a room that should have been familiar to her. Then her gaze fell on him, and his body tightened with such swiftness that for a heartbeat he felt lightheaded, dizzy. He should look away, tell her with an averted glance that she was nothing to him, that he had no interest in her; and yet he seemed incapable of doing anything other than watch as she hesitantly strolled toward him.

Finally she was standing before him, her small gloved hands folded tightly in front of her. With her this near to him, he could see clearly that her eyes were the most beautiful blue. No, more than blue. Violet. He'd never seen the like. He imagined them smoldering, darkening with desire, gazing at him in wonder as he delivered pleasure such as she'd never experienced. An easy task if she had indeed never known a man's touch.

But just as he had no use for mistresses, so he had none for virgins. He had not been innocent in a good long while. He had no interest in innocence. It was a weakness, a condition to be exploited, a quick path to ruin. It held no appeal.

She held no appeal.

He rethought the words in an attempt to convince himself of their truth. But as her eyes bore into his, he was left with the realization that she was not only innocent, but very, very dangerous. A silly thought. He could destroy her with a look, a word, a caustic laugh. And in destroying her, the tiny bit of soul that remained in him would wither and die.

It was an unsettling realization, one he didn't much like.

He watched her delicate throat work as she swallowed, her bosom rise with the intake of a long breath as though she were shoring up her courage.

"I don't believe we've spoken," she finally said.

"No."

"May I inquire regarding your name? The other gentlemen were kind enough to introduce themselves."

"But then I am not kind."

Two tiny pleats appeared between her brows. "Why would you say something of that nature?"

"Because I *am* honest, at least."

"But surely you have a name. Is it a secret? You steal children from their beds? Rumpelstiltskin, perhaps? I would be hard-pressed to see you as Prince Charming."

Fairy tales. She'd been brought up on fairy tales, and she seemed to have no awareness that she was wading through a nest of ogres.

"Come. It can't be that horrible of a name. I'd like to call you something."

He considered suggesting Beelzebub, something to unsettle her, send her scurrying away, but for reasons he couldn't fathom he simply said, "Rafe."

"Rafe," she repeated in her smoky voice and a fierce longing fissured through him with an almost painful pricking. "Is that your title?"

"No."

"Are you titled?"

Perhaps she wasn't as innocent as he'd surmised. She wanted to ensure that she was well cared for, was going to be particular about whose bed she warmed. He supposed he couldn't hold that against her. She was on the hunt for a man to please, one who would serve as her protector. She had a right to be particular.

"No," he finally answered.

"I see you're a man of few words." She gnawed on her lower lip, which served to plump it up and darken its red hue. He wondered how often she'd been kissed. Had she ever let a man press his mouth to hers? Had a man ever touched her skin, trailed his fingers along her high cheekbones, folded his rough hand around her neck, and brought her in close? "What are your interests?"

"None that would amuse you."

"You might be surprised."

"I doubt it. I'm a rather good judge of character."

"A quick judge, it would seem. I'm left with the impression that you don't think very highly of me."

He slid his gaze over her, admiring the curves, dips, and swells. He couldn't deny that she was a fine piece, but she would require a certain ... gentleness and care, neither of which was in his repertoire of behavior. "I haven't decided."

"Unfortunately I have, I'm afraid. I don't believe we'd be well suited. I hope you won't take offense."

"I would have to give a care what you thought to be offended. I don't."

She opened her mouth—

"Evelyn, you're done here," Wortham said, suddenly at her side. He grabbed her arm and began madly ushering her toward the door.

Almost tripping over her small feet encased in satin slippers, she appeared to be attempting to shake off the earl. She was gazing over her bared shoulder at Rafe as though she was determined to have the final word, but she was no match for Wortham's strength as they both disappeared through the open doorway. It was some minutes before Wortham returned. Rafe was surprised Miss Chambers didn't barge in behind him. No doubt he'd dissuaded her, so as not to discourage any of the lords from having an interest in her.

"All right, gentlemen," Wortham said, rubbing his hands together. "Does anyone wish to bid on her?"

So that was how he was going to handle the matter, Rafe mused. He'd wondered. He didn't know why the manner in which Wortham was proceeding caused a chill in his bones. The girl meant nothing to him. It might prove interesting to see what sort of value the other lords placed on her, especially if he could determine a way to use that knowledge to his advantage.

"I say, Wortham," Lord Ekroth sneered, "I'll give you five hundred quid for her, but I've a mind to examine her first and ensure she is a virgin as you claim."

A round of raucous laughter accompanied the ribald suggestion. Rafe suspected those who laughed the loudest were striving to cover the fact that they weren't quite comfortable with the direction in which the evening was going.

"By all means. Each of you may examine her," Wortham said callously as though he were offering little more than a mare for purchase. "Then I shall entertain further bids."

"Excellent. I'll go first, shall I?" He and Wortham headed for the door.

Rafe envisioned Ekroth's pudgy, sausage-like fingers traveling over her silky thighs, ripping at her undergarments, shoving into—

"I'm taking her." Rafe could hardly countenance the words that burst from his own mouth with such authority that Ekroth and Wortham stumbled in their tracks, while the other lords gaped at him. Obviously, he'd imbibed a bit more than he'd thought, but it didn't matter now. The challenge had been spoken, and he never recanted his statements.

Standing, he tugged on his black brocade waistcoat that suddenly felt far too tight. "If any of you touch her, I shall separate from you the particular part that touched her. Wortham has assured us that she is pure. I don't want her soiled by your sweaty hands or anything else. Have I made myself clear?"

"But you were only here to watch, to ascertain"— Wortham cut off his sentence and stepped nearer, lowering his voice—"to ascertain my ability to cover my debt."

"When have I ever confided my plans in you?"

"Then you'll pay me the five hundred quid that Ekroth was willing to pony up?"

"I'll allow you to continue to breathe. We'll call it even, shall we?"

"But the terms of this meeting were that she would go to the highest bidder."

"What value do you place on your life? Do you think anyone here can match it?" He waited a heartbeat. "I thought not."

He downed what remained of his Scotch before striding to the desk, lords leaping out of his way. If he were not a stranger to laughter, he might have at least chuckled at their antics. He found a scrap of paper, dipped a pen in the inkwell, and scratched out the address of his residence. Putting a blotter on it to keep it in place, he turned and headed toward the door. "My address. Have her there at four tomorrow. Good evening, gentlemen. As always, it's been a pleasure to be in such esteemed company."

He was in his carriage, traveling through the London streets, before it resonated within him exactly what he'd done.

"Good God," he muttered, even though no one was about to hear. What the devil had he been thinking? Obviously, he hadn't.

He glared out the window at the fog-shrouded night. His taking her had nothing to do with the fact that she was in effect being abandoned, because she wasn't. She was being given to someone to care for her. She wouldn't go hungry, she wouldn't be smacked about, she wouldn't have to work until her fingers bled and the small of her back ached so hideously that she feared she might never be able to straighten. She would lie in silk on beds and fainting couches and wait for a man to part her thighs. She would eat chocolates and plump her lips. She would run her tongue around those lips and gaze at her benefactor through half-lowered lids.

And he was her benefactor. Damnation.

He should have allowed Ekroth to have her. His fingers weren't all that pudgy. He could call on him in the morning, barter, let him take her.

But then he'd appear to be a man who didn't know his own mind.

So he was stuck with her. For a time, anyway.

Perhaps it wouldn't be so awful. She'd never had a man. He could guide her toward pleasing him in the manner he required. She would have no other experience, so she would know nothing different, and therefore she would not be disappointed.

The possibilities began to have merit. He didn't have to care about her. He wouldn't care about her.

But he could damn well make use of her.

ABOUT THE AUTHOR

LORRAINE HEATH wrote her first story at age ten, and it involved a dashing ... hero who fell in love with ... She has since moved on to writing more sexy cowboys and dashing English lords (and sometimes, devoted to the same book). *Publishers Weekly* says she is a "master of her craft." She is married, and along with being a *New York Times* and *USA Today* bestseller, she has won the RITA Award, four *Romantic Times Reviewers' Choice Awards*, and a *Romantic Times Career Achievement Award*.

Visit www.AuthorTracker.com for exclusive information on your favorite HarperCollins authors.

Give in to your impulses . . .
Read on for a sneak peek at five brand-new
e-book original tales of romance
from Avon Books.
Available now wherever e-books are sold.

NIGHTS OF STEEL
THE ETHER CHRONICLES
By Nico Rosso

ALICE'S WONDERLAND
By Allison Dobell

ONE FINE FIREMAN
A BACHELOR FIREMEN NOVELLA
By Jennifer Bernard

THERE'S SOMETHING
ABOUT LADY MARY

A SUMMERSBY TALE

By Sophie Barnes

THE SECRET LIFE OF LADY LUCINDA

A SUMMERSBY TALE

By Sophie Barnes

An Excerpt from

NIGHTS OF STEEL

The Ether Chronicles

by Nico Rosso

**Return to The Ether Chronicles, where
rival bounty hunters Anna Blue and Jack
Hawkins join forces to find a mysterious
fugitive, only to get so much more than they
bargained for. The skies above the American
West are about to get wilder than ever . . .**

Take his hand? Or walk down the broken stairs to chase a cold trail. Anna's body was still buffeted by waves of sensation. The meal was an adventure she shared with Jack. Nearly falling from the stairs, only to be brought close to his body, had been a rush. The hissing of the lodge was the last bit of danger, but it had passed.

The wet heat of that simple room was inviting. Her joints

and bones ached for comfort. Deeper down, she yearned for Jack. They'd been circling each other for years. The closer she got—hearing his voice, touching his skin, learning his history—the more the hunger increased. She didn't know where it would lead her, but she had to find out. All she had to do was take his hand.

Anna slid her palm against his. Curled her fingers around him. He held her hand, staring into her eyes. She'd thought she knew the man behind the legend and the metal and the guns, yet now she understood there were miles of territory within him she had yet to discover.

Their grips tightened. They drew closer. He leaned down to her. She pressed against his chest. In the sunlight, they kissed. Neither hid their hunger. She understood his need. His lips on hers were strong, devouring. And she understood her yearning. Probing forward with her tongue, she led him into her.

And it wasn't enough. Their first kiss could've taken them too far and she'd had to stop. Now, with Jack pressed against her, his arm wrapped around her shoulders and his lips against hers, too far seemed like the perfect place to go.

They pulled apart and, each still gripping the other's hand, walked back into the lodge room. Sheets of steam curled up the walls and filled the space, bringing out the scent of the redwood paneling. The room seemed alive, breathing with her.

Jack cracked a small smile. "This guy, Song, I like his style. Lot of inventors are drunk on tetrol. Half-baked ideas that don't work right." He held up his half-mechanical hand. "People wind up getting hurt."

"Song knows his business," she agreed. "So why the bounty?"

He leveled his gaze at her. It seemed the steam came from him, his intensity. "You want a cold trail or a hot bath?"

She took off her hat, holding his look and not backing down. "Hot. Bath."

Burbling invitingly like a secluded brook, the tub waited in the corner. The steam softened its edges and obscured the walls around it. As if the room went on forever.

With the toe of his boot, Jack swung the front door closed. Only the small lights in the ceiling glowed. Warm night clouds now surrounded her. A gentle storm. And Jack was the lightning. Still gripping her hand, he walked her toward the tub, chuckling a little to himself.

"My last bath was at a lonely little stage stop hotel in Camarillo."

The buckle on her gun belt was hot from the steam. "I'm overdue." She undid it and held the rig in her hand.

"I'm guessing you picked up Malone's trail sometime after the Sierras, so it's been a few hundred miles for you, too."

It took her a second to track her path backward. "Beatty, Nevada."

"Rough town." He let go of her hand so he could undo the straps and belts that held his own weapons.

She hung her gun belt on a wooden peg on the wall next to the tub. Easy to reach if she had to. "A little less rough after I left."

His pistols and quad shotgun took their place next to her weapons. He was unarmed. But still deadly. Broad shoulders, muscled arms and legs. Dark, blazing eyes. And the smallest smile.

They came together again, this time without the clang of gunmetal. The heat of the room had soaked through her clothes, bringing a light sweat across her skin. She felt every fold of fabric, and every ridge of his muscles. Her hands ran over the cords of his neck, pulling him to her mouth for another kiss.

Nerves yearned for sensation. Dust storms had chafed her flesh. Ice-cold rivers had woken her up, and she'd slept in the rain while waiting out a fugitive. She needed pleasure. And Jack was the only man strong enough to bring it to her.

An Excerpt from

ALICE'S WONDERLAND
by Allison Dobell

When journalist and notorious womanizer
Flynn O'Grady publicly mocks Alice Mitchell's
erotic luxury goods website, the game is on. They
soon find themselves locked in a sensual battle
where Alice must step up the spice night after
night as, one by one, Flynn's defenses crumble.

AN AVON RED NOVELLA

Flynn O'Grady had gone too far this time. It was bad enough
that Sydney Daily's resident male blogger continued to push
his low opinions about women into the community (he
seemed to have an ongoing problem with shoes and shopping), but this time he'd mentioned her business by name.

How dare he suggest she was a charlatan, promising the

world and delivering nothing! The women who came to Alice's Wonderland were discerning, educated, and thoroughly in charge of their sexuality. They loved to play and knew the value in paying for quality. They knew the difference between her beautiful artisan-made, hand-carved, silver-handled spanking paddle (of which she'd moved over 500 units this past financial year, she might add) and a $79.95 mass-produced Taiwanese purple plastic dildo from hihosilver.com.

Still, while Alice didn't agree with the raunch culture that prevailed at hihosilver, she'd defend (with one of their cheap dildos raised high) the right of any woman to take on a Tickler, Rabbit, or Climax Gem in the privacy of her own home. Where was it written that men had cornered the market for liking sex? O'Grady had clearly been under a rock for at least three decades.

Alice reached for the old-fashioned cream-and-gold telephone on her glass-topped desk and dialed. She knew what she needed to do to make a man like Flynn O'Grady understand where she was coming from. As the phone rang, she re-read the blog entry for the third time. Anger rose within her, but she pushed it down. She'd need her wits about her for this conversation.

"O'Grady."

Alice took a deep breath before she began. "Mr. O'Grady, we haven't met, but you seem to know all about me."

A brief silence on the other end.

"I see," came the answer. "Would you care to elaborate?" His voice was deep and husky around the edges. He should have been in radio, rather than in print.

"Alice Mitchell here. Purveyor of broken promises."

Another pause.

"Ms. Mitchell, how . . . delightful." His tone made it clear that it was anything but.

"I'm sure," said Alice, raising one eyebrow slightly, allowing her smile to warm her words. "You've had quite a lot to say about my business today. I was wondering if we could meet. I think I deserve the right of reply."

"I'm not sure what good that would do, Ms. Mitchell," he replied, smoothly. "You're more than welcome to respond via the comments section on my blog."

She'd had the feeling he'd try that.

"I think this is more . . . personal than that," Alice purred down the line. "I'd like to try to convince you of my . . . position." She stifled a laugh, enjoying every second of this. She could easily imagine him squirming in his chair right now.

The silence that followed inched toward uncomfortable.

"Er, right. Well, I don't have any time today, but I could see you on Wednesday," he said.

It was Monday. Give him all day Tuesday to plan his defenses? Not likely.

"It would be great if you could make it today," she said, a hint of steel entering her tone. "I'd hate to have to take this to your boss. I suspect there may be grounds for a defamation complaint, but I'm sure the two of us can work it out . . ." She left the idea dangling. The media was no place for job insecurity in the current climate, and she knew he was too smart not to know that. He needed to keep his boss happy.

"I could fit you in tonight, but it would need to be after 7.30," he said, his voice carefully controlled.

'"Perfect," she said, "I'll come to your office."

She put down the phone, allowing him no time to answer, then sat back in her chair. Now all she needed to do was select an item or two that would help her to convince Flynn he should change his mind.

Standing quickly, she prowled over to the open glass shelving that took up one wall of her domain. Although it might be of use in getting her point across, it was probably too soon for the geisha gag. She didn't know him well enough to bring out the tooled leather slave-style handcuffs. Wait a minute! She almost spanked herself with the paddle that Flynn O'Grady had derided for overlooking the obvious.

Moving to a small glass cabinet in the corner, she opened the top drawer and inspected the silken blindfolds. She picked up a scarlet one and held it, delicate and cool to the touch, in her hand.

Perfect.

An Excerpt from

ONE FINE FIREMAN

A BACHELOR FIREMEN NOVELLA

by Jennifer Bernard

**What happens when you mix together an
absolutely gorgeous fireman, a beautiful but
shy woman, her precocious kid, and
a very mischievous little dog? Find out in
Jennifer Bernard's sizzling hot *One Fine Fireman*.**

The door opened, and three firemen walked in. Maribel
nearly dropped the Lazy Morning Specials in table six's lap.
Goodness, they were like hand grenades of testosterone rolling in the door, sucking all the air out of the room. They wore
dark blue t-shirts tucked into their yellow firemen's pants, thick
suspenders holding up the trousers. They walked with rolling
strides, probably because of their big boots. Individually they
were handsome, but collectively they were devastating.

Maribel knew most of the San Gabriel firemen by name. The brown-haired one with eyes the color of a summer day was Ryan Blake. The big, bulky guy with the intimidating muscles was called Vader. She had no idea what his real name was, but apparently the nickname came from the way he loved to make spooky voices with his breathing apparatus. The third one trailed behind the others, and she couldn't make out his identity. Then Ryan took a step forward, revealing the man behind him. She sucked in a breath.

Kirk was back. For months she'd been wondering where he was and been too shy to ask. She'd worried that he'd transferred to another town, or decided to chuck it all and sail around the world. She'd been half afraid she'd never see him again. But here he was, in the flesh, just as mouthwatering as ever. Her face heated as she darted glance after glance at him, like a starving person just presented with prime rib. It was wrong, so wrong; she was engaged. But she couldn't help it. She had to see if everything about him was as she remembered.

His silvery gray-green eyes, the exact color of the sagebrush that grew in the hills around San Gabriel, hadn't changed, though he looked more tired than she remembered. His blond hair, which he'd cut drastically since she'd last seen him, picked up glints of sunshine through the plate glass window. His face looked thinner, maybe older, a little pale. But his mouth still had that secret humorous quirk. The rest of his face usually held a serious expression, but his mouth told a different story. It was as if he hid behind a quiet mask, but his mouth had chosen to rebel. Not especially tall, he had a powerful, quiet presence and a spectacular physique under his firefighter gear. She noticed that, unlike the others, he wore a long-sleeved shirt.

His fellow firefighters called him Thor. She could certainly see why. He looked like her idea of a Viking god, though she would imagine the God of Thunder would be more of a loudmouth. Kirk was not a big talker. He didn't say much, but when he spoke, people seemed to listen.

She certainly did, even though all he'd said to her was, "Black, no sugar," and "How much are those little Christmas ornaments?" referring to the beaded angels she made for sale during the holidays. It was embarrassing how much she relived those little moments afterward.

Tossing friendly smiles to the other customers, the three men strolled to the counter where she took the orders. They gathered around the menu board, though why they bothered, she didn't know. They always ordered the same thing. Firemen seemed to be creatures of habit. Or at least her firemen were.

An Excerpt from

THERE'S SOMETHING ABOUT LADY MARY

A SUMMERSBY TALE

by Sophie Barnes

When Mary Croyden inherits a title and a
large sum of money, she must rely on the help
of one man—Ryan Summersby. But Mary's
hobbies are not exactly proper, and Ryan is
starting to realize that this simple miss is
not at all what he expected . . . in the second
Summersby Tale from Sophie Barnes.

Mary stepped back. Had she really forgotten to introduce
herself? Was it possible that Ryan Summersby didn't know
who she really was? She suddenly dreaded having to tell him.
She'd enjoyed spending time with him, had even considered
the possibility of seeing him again, but once he knew her true

identity, he'd probably treat her no differently than all the other gentlemen had done—like a grand pile of treasure with which to pay off his debts and house his mistresses.

Squaring her shoulders and straightening her spine, she mustered all her courage and turned a serious gaze upon him. "My name is Mary Croyden, and I am the Marchioness of Steepleton."

Ryan's response was instantaneous. His mouth dropped open while his eyes widened in complete and utter disbelief. He stared at the slender woman who stood before him, doing her best to play the part of a peeress. Was it really possible that she was the very marchioness he'd been looking for when he'd stepped outside for some fresh air only half an hour earlier? The very same one that Percy had asked him to protect? She seemed much too young for such a title, too unpolished. It wasn't that he found her unattractive in any way, though he had thought her plain at first glance.

"What?" she asked, as she crossed her arms and cocked an eyebrow. "Not what you expected the infamous Marchioness of Steepleton to look like?"

"Not exactly, no," he admitted. "You are just not—"

"Not what? Not pretty enough? Not sophisticated enough? Or is it perhaps that the way in which I speak fails to equate with your ill-conceived notion of what a marchioness ought to sound like?" He had no chance to reply before she said, "Well, you do not exactly strike me as a stereotypical medical student either."

"And just what exactly would you know about that?" he asked, a little put out by her sudden verbal attack.

"Enough," she remarked in a rather clipped tone. "My

father was a skilled physician. I know the sort of man it takes to fill such a position, and you, my lord, do not fit the bill."

For the first time in his life, Ryan Summersby found himself at a complete loss for words. Not only could he not comprehend that this slip of a woman before him, appearing to be barely out of the schoolroom, was a peeress in her own right—not to mention a woman of extreme wealth. But that she was actually standing there, fearlessly scolding him . . . he knew that a sane person would be quite offended, and yet he couldn't help but be enthralled.

In addition, he'd also managed to glimpse a side of her that he very much doubted many people had ever seen. "You do not think too highly of yourself, do you?" He suddenly asked.

That brought her up short. "I have no idea what you could possibly mean by that," she told him defensively.

"Well, you assume that I do not believe you to be who you say you are. You think the reasoning behind my not believing you might have something to do with the way you look. Finally, you feel the need to assert yourself by finding fault with me—for which I must commend you, since I do not have very many faults at all."

"You arrogant . . ." The marchioness wisely clamped her mouth shut before uttering something that she would be bound to regret. Instead, she turned away and walked toward the French doors that led toward the ballroom. "Thank you for the dance, Mr. Summersby. I hope you enjoy the rest of your evening," she called over her shoulder in an obvious attempt at sounding dignified.

"May I call on you sometime?" he asked, ignoring her

abrupt dismissal of him as he thought of the task that Percy had given him. It really wouldn't do for him to muck things up so early in the game. And besides, he wasn't sure he'd ever met a woman who interested him more than Lady Steepleton did at that very moment. He had to admit that the woman had character.

She paused in the middle of her exit, turned slightly, and looked him dead in the eye. "You most certainly may not, Mr. Summersby." And before Ryan had a chance to dispute the matter, she had vanished back inside, the white cotton of her gown twirling about her feet.

An Excerpt from

THE SECRET LIFE OF LADY LUCINDA

A SUMMERSBY TALE

by Sophie Barnes

Lucy Blackwell throws caution to the wind
when she tricks Lord William Summersby
into a marriage of convenience. But she
never counted on falling in love . . .

"Do you love her?" Miss Blackwell suddenly asked, her head
tilted upward at a slight angle.

Lord, even her voice was delightful to listen to. And those
imploring eyes of hers . . . No, he'd be damned if he'd allow
her to ensnare him with her womanly charms. She'd practi-
cally made fools of both his sister and his father—she'd get
no sympathy from him. Not now, not ever. "You and I are
hardly well enough acquainted with one another for you to
take such liberties in your questions, Miss Blackwell. My

relationship to Lady Annabelle is of a personal nature, and certainly not one that I am about to discuss with you."

Miss Blackwell blinked. "Then you do not love her," she said simply.

"I hold her in the highest regard," he said.

Miss Blackwell stared back at him with an increased measure of doubt in her eyes. "More reason for me to believe that you do not love her."

"Miss Blackwell, if I did not know any better, I should say that you are either mad or deaf—perhaps even both. At no point have I told you that I do not love her, yet you are quite insistent upon the matter."

"That is because, my lord, it is in everything you are saying and everything that you are not. If you truly loved her, you would not have had a moment's hesitation in professing it. It is therefore my belief that you do not love her but are marrying her simply out of obligation."

Why the blazes he was having this harebrained conversation with a woman he barely even knew, much less liked, was beyond him. But the beginnings of a smile that now played upon her lips did nothing short of make him catch his breath. With a sigh of resignation, he slowly nodded his head. "Well done, Miss Blackwell. You have indeed found me out."

Her smile broadened. "Then it really doesn't matter whom you marry, as long as you marry. Is that not so?"

He frowned, immediately on guard at her sudden enthusiasm. "Not exactly, no. The woman I marry must be one of breeding, of a gentle nature and graceful bearing. Lady Annabelle fits all of those criteria rather nicely, and, in time, I am more than confident that we shall become quite fond of one another."

The impossible woman had the audacity to roll her eyes. "All I really wanted to know was whether or not anyone's heart might be jeopardized if you were persuaded to marry somebody else. That is all."

"Miss Blackwell, I can assure you that I have no intention of marrying anyone other than Lady Annabelle. She and I have a mutual agreement. We are both honorable people. Neither one of us would ever consider going back on his word."

"I didn't think as much," she mused, and before William had any time to consider what she might be about to do, she'd thrown her arms around his neck, pulled him toward her, and placed her lips against his.